ex libris

More books by Elizabeth Watasin

The Dark Victorian: Risen Vol 1
The Dark Victorian: Bones Vol 2

Ice Demon: A Dark Victorian Penny Dread Vol 1

Sundark: An Elle Black Penny Dread

Charm School Graphique Vol 1

MEDUSA

A Dark Victorian Penny Dread
Volume Two

By
Elizabeth Watasin

A-GIRL STUDIO

Medusa: A Dark Victorian Penny Dread Volume Two
Copyright © 2015 by Elizabeth Watasin
All rights reserved.

An A-Girl Studio book
published 2015 in the USA.

For additional information, please contact:
A-Girl Studio
P.O. Box 213, Burbank, CA 91503 U.S.A.
www.a-girlstudio.com

ISBN: 978-1-936622-24-5
Library of Congress Control Number:
2015901211
First paperback edition, 2015

❖

Cover design and art by Elizabeth Watasin
And
Phatpuppy Creations
phatpuppyart.com
Cover model is Elizabeth Worth
www.modelmayhem.com/3122503
Custom Wardrobe Creation: Cavalyn Galano
www.facebook.com/CavalynDesign
Makeup/Hair: Nadya Rutman
www.bynadya.com
Photography: Teresa Yeh Photography
teresayeh.com
Typography by Tom Orzechowski and Lois Buhalis
serifsup.com

Editing by JoSelle Vanderhooft
www.joselle-vanderhooft.com

Medusa head illustration after Walter Crane

*Dedicated
to
the
differently
Aware*

The main thing is to be moved, to love, to hope, to tremble, to live.
— Auguste Rodin

CHAPTER ONE

In sedate Bloomsbury, two blind women, one tall and one small, walked up the grand portico steps of the bustling British Museum and entered. Both wore opaque, black spectacles with round lenses and carried walking sticks, the taller woman's of sturdy blackthorn studded with silver pieces, and the smaller woman's of slender, white, diamond willow. Petite Elvie Chaisty, then twenty-six years of age and happily independent, linked arms with her lanky companion and matched Ellie Hench's confident, longer stride while listening to the noises and footsteps near them. She extended her aural focus for the multitudinous echoes returning from the high dome, which gave her the familiar yet daunting impression of the British Museum's cavernous spaciousness. To move within a cacophony where she could easily be lost was overwhelming, yet exciting.

As she and the other Institute of the Blind boarders had practiced, she held her chin up. Not only did it command attention from sighted people, it also kept the neck muscles from weakening. And Elvie was proud to hold her head high, even if it meant startling passersby with a glimpse of her fleshy eye sockets behind her black lenses and half-closed lids. When rude children asked where her eyeballs had gone, Elvie would explain that she'd entirely misplaced them and all that was left was the muscle and tissue that had sat behind them. If the children were especially rude, she told them that a troll had climbed through her bedroom window and eaten them, and that they had better watch out lest he ate theirs next.

She heard Ellie trip someone with her blackthorn—a foot gave a resounding clap upon the marble floor, and then the person ejected a startled apology, at which she suppressed a smile. If Ellie tripped sighted people, it was because they didn't move out of her and Elvie's path fast enough.

Ellie still possessed her eyeballs, though they had never worked in the conventional manner. She was blind but could still "see" their world with a gift preternatural. What little scientific scrutiny Ellie had allowed on herself had been at a loss to define her abilities. She'd described her acuity as her perceiving the components of their world like a giant eyeball. It inhaled the flow of the world's "fluid" and breathed back out recognition of all the elements within that fluid, to their exact measure. People and objects were clear to her perceptions, right down to the tiniest planes of their surfaces. Such precision also meant that Ellie knew exactly how to strike someone, thus making her a very deadly stick for hire. She earned a good wage as a bodyguard for women, and Elvie was perfectly happy to use her escorting services.

They passed the great central area housing the Reading Room, libraries, and Department of Manuscripts—places Ellie helped her to visit (the whispers and studious silences in the Reading Room were delightful to experience, though frustrating, since Elvie could not participate in such research)—then meandered through the crowded wing where the Roman, Greek, Hellenistic, Assyrian, and Egyptian galleries resided. All such rooms and places gave the same noises to Elvie, and she only knew what they passed when Ellie announced the rooms to her—though Ellie was prone to assuming all Roman objects were Greek and anything with paws or wearing very tall hats was Egyptian. Despite Ellie's abilities, a sign with printed words was still just a flat sign with flat markings, and these communications of the sighted were what her perceptions could not discern.

However, only one room interested Elvie; of all the museum's precious contents, stored behind glass and within locked cases—the gems, medals, treasures, mummies, marbles, coins, minerals, botanicals, and taxidermic species—she was allowed to touch nothing except for the artefacts in a certain basement gallery. It was a place set aside for fine-art students and blind visitors: Room 84, the storage gallery for lesser Roman antiquities.

"Stairs now, Elvie," Ellie said. "Down we go. One. . . ."

Elvie picked up her skirts and felt Ellie drop down. She put out her foot and also hit the step below.

"Two," Ellie said and stepped down again, Elvie joining. "Three."

Elvie matched the rhythm of Ellie's descending steps, and thus they moved down to the basement of the British Museum.

When they reached the hall and approached the room, Elvie held Ellie's arm tighter in anticipation and set her willow down to tap about. Unlike Ellie, she was prone to trip far too many people and not on purpose. She heard no other footsteps but theirs echo in the hall. Ellie brought her to a stop and she knew then that they stood before the entrance of the sculpture gallery. They paused in silence, and Elvie heard the distant, faint scratch of marks being made on paper. She listened harder, trying to discern where the person was in the room.

"Yer in luck, Elvie, no custodian in attendance to pester you."

"Not even in hiding to peep at me?"

"If he's behind one of them columns, 'e has to breathe sometime."

Elvie squeezed Ellie's arm and smiled, relieved.

"You were right to come with me a third time, just to make certain I'm truly free of him. Is there more than the one I hear—fine-art students, perhaps?" she said.

"No more are within, unless they're hidin' in the marble sarcophagi. Just the one, a young girl, and she sits before yer nymph, Elvie. She's drawing 'er."

"I must wait to visit my favourite, then. Has anything new arrived?"

"I haven't this room mapped like you, Elvie, but I did count those disc throwers once," Ellie said, "when I was bored. There are five now, and the new fellow's just ahead of us."

"A new *discobolus*? Oh, bring me to him!"

Ellie led her down one aisle, its path uneven due to the haphazard positioning of the stored statues. Some sat on bases, others not, which made it easier for Elvie to reach for their faces. She had needed many visits to memorise which marble thrust out hands, swords, or spread wings that her own face might bump into. There, was the plump putto; next was a colossal foot. Then came the headless woman holding a spear, and after her, the leaning youth draped with a goatskin. By knowing each landmark, Elvie could expand her measure of the space and understand its dimensions and her place in it. If anyone were to ask if she knew of the rooms and halls beyond where she stood, or even where her floor was situated within the entirety of the building, she would have to admit she did not, for she and her fellow blind only best understood the makings of their immediate surroundings.

The landscape of Room 84 would change when new marbles arrived or others disappeared, for the gallery was the lodging place of the more inferior Roman copies of Greek bronzes. Also stored were alleged forgeries, incorrect restorations, and, as one curator had noted, the "less-loved" donations from the collections of deceased antiquarians. Ellie brought Elvie to a halt and raised Elvie's hand. She placed it on a cool, smooth marble surface. It was the shoulder of the new *discobolus*.

"Feel that, Elvie? He's your height, not so very big, and stands next to that patriarch bust, the one you call 'Sophocles.'"

"Oh, that's not his true name."

"Well, why do you call 'im that, Elvie?"

"Because in the ancient magical world, true names have the power of summoning, Petronella," Elvie said in humour.

Ellie huffed. "I'm already 'ere, Elfin, so no need to summon me twice. Sophy is to yer left. You should know yer way from there."

Elvie rested her stick against the *discobolus* and laid both hands on his twisting back. Ellie moved away and then fussed with her skirts, as if seating herself. Elvie heard a book opened and the smooth *shuff* of a page being turned.

Then there was another soft, scoring sound, of Ellie's fingers tracing along the braille dots of the page. Elvie ran her palms down the stone.

"Such a dull recreation," she observed. "A bored *practicien* chiselled these unremarkable buttocks."

"I once went dancin' with a physical culturist," Ellie said. "All of muscles. Now there was a man with buttocks to remark upon."

"Were they so very firm?"

"A rump fit for Christmas dinner, Elvie."

Elvie moved around the marble and trailed her hands up to explore his neck and found an almost indiscernible seam that ran from his throat to the nape. She traced it. "His head's been reattached, Ellie, and it must be his new one, for it's all wrong. He's meant to look towards his discus, not away. And how characterless are his features. It's a halfhearted restoration, at best."

Ellie gave no answer. Elvie heard another page turn. But while she took further stock of the new *discobolus*'s limbs and other surfaces (for her personal mental catalogue, for she fancied herself the unofficial curator of the gallery's contents), she became aware of a pervading fragrance.

My, so it is this artist who wears that perfume, Elvie thought.

It was a lush, floral scent, the seductive power of roses. But that heady aroma was a pleasing layer cloaking a more profound odour; a richer, piercing fragrance mixed with a subtler, deeper bitter tone. A Chinese apothecary had introduced it to her once, naming it the "calling-back-the-soul" fragrance.

"Frankincense with myrrh," Elvie whispered.

She knew the rose scent from a previous visit; it lingered

in her senses and imagination long after she and Ellie had left for the day. Ellie had said that the artist present was a young girl; how wrong the scent seemed for her. Right then Elvie could hear the scratching of her earnest sketching, its struggled movements sounding less assured than the more learned, swift hands she'd listened to in the National Gallery, made by the woman painters who earned a modest sum covertly copying museum masterworks for clients. The beguiling, complex fragrance seemed fit for a woman of queenly stature and not, she presumptuously assumed, for one still maturing into a princess.

I won't approach her, Elvie thought with disappointment. The young artist might be a mature soul, but Elvie had hoped to meet a grown woman in possession of such an intriguing scent, not a girl.

She left the unremarkable *discobolus* copy and laid a hand on the marble next to him. It was the stern bust of a bald, bearded patriarch, her "Sophocles." Thus orientated, she touched her careful way to a fragmented recreation nearby, replicated at a far smaller scale than the original it emulated, or so a curator had told her. Elvie placed her hands on the straining chest of the *Laocoön* and ran her fingers down his cool marble torso. She marvelled again at the shapes of his abdomen muscles, then reached over to his veined hand that clenched the thick body of a snake coiled around his tense arm. Its wide jaws were set to snap at his hip, an everlasting threat of the bite of death. Elvie shivered, as she always did when grasping the snake's deadly head. She then moved her hand lower.

"When you giggle like that, Elvie, I know you're touchin' some poor marble's spouter," Ellie remarked.

"Well, it is the *Laocoön*'s, Ellie. His parts are all intact, and so informative."

Ellie hummed in response and turned another page of her book. Elvie heard skirts shuffle as a body rose. Tools clattered, and a case snapped closed.

"Good day to you both," a girl called.

"Good day," Ellie pleasantly replied. Elvie heard skirt fabric brush against stone and move away. "Well now, Elvie, your nymph is free for yer company."

Elvie smiled. She heard another page turn, then made her determined way to the marble the young artist had abandoned.

Ellie flipped the pages of her book but only pretended to read. Chin raised, hat cocked, and her typical half-grin upon her lips, her attention was focused solely on a new presence in the room. The visitor had entered so silently that Elvie had not even detected her, and once the student had left, she had glided just as silently to a spot where Elvie, facing Ellie, stood oblivious between them.

One advantage to masquerading as fully blind was that Ellie could read her braille and "read" her surroundings; those present would never know that she was watching them. On her first visit accompanying Elvie, the custodian of the room had quietly approached Elvie right in Ellie's presence, placed his hand where he should not upon his trousers, and, as Ellie expected he would when she confronted him, protested his innocence. She could not prove what she'd witnessed, because as the man's embarrassed superior had pointed out, she had to have heard what the man did with his hand, and wouldn't she, a blind woman, be mistaken about what that might be? Then, on the last visit, the custodian had hidden behind a column to watch Elvie.

When Elvie had called for her, alarmed at the sound of heavy breathing, it was reason enough to chase the pest out, knock him between the legs, and give formal complaint to his superior. She apologised to Elvie for making her endure more vulgar attentions, but her having heard his actions gave proof to the formal complaint (and an excuse to beat more upon him).

During the incident of the heavy breathing, the current visitor in the room had been present, just as silently as before, standing behind the oblivious custodian while he watched Elvie and touched himself. Ellie didn't know why the woman had not reacted, though she nearly suspected that their observer was, in truth, waiting for some right moment to *do* something. After the chasing of the custodian, the woman had disappeared, and Ellie had filed her away as a distinction to note. For the woman, indeed, was quite distinct.

Right then, the visitor did not seem cognisant that Ellie was aware of her. The fluidity of their world gave Ellie the precise details of their visitor: she was well-dressed, upper class, and half-obscured by a column she'd chosen to stand behind. Her revealed half was of a tall, well-formed, feminine body with loose hair gathered in a tight, opaque snood. By the standards of their day, the strong figure she cut might be described as handsome. At her one eye was a protruding monocle, one mounted into a mask covering the upper half of her face.

Wonder what 'orribleness she's concealing, Ellie thought. *Like Helia.*

And like Helia Skycourt, there was a life-glow to the woman that spoke of some eldritch taint, though Ellie thought it inaccurate to call it such. Instead, the woman's life-fire seemed made of something otherworldly entirely.

Rather like that ghost agent, Artifice, Ellie thought. *Who's wholly nothing ordinary.*

Ellie turned another page of her book and decided, for the moment, to let the woman continue her scrutiny.

The woman's statuelike stillness gave the impression of practiced covertness, though the invisibility act failed to escape Ellie's unique sense of detection. Eldritch the woman might be, but she was not a gruesome reanimation or some aspect of undead—like the vampyres, whose life-glow Ellie could only explain as that which seemed reversed. Ellie discerned living warmth—a being of true flesh—and the soft, subtle disturbance that breath made in the liquidity of their fluid world. Even breath slowed and made to come as quietly as the woman was then breathing was still evidence of something living.

The stranger's attention appeared to be upon them, though if Ellie's senses could discern eyeballs and the direction of such eyes (and this, she could not, for it had something to do with pupils, which were mere flat things to her), she could affirm her ascertainment that the woman's gaze dwelled solely upon Elvie.

Ellie ran her fingers along her lines of braille and marked how she might reach Elvie should the woman choose to approach her.

The woman wore an odd decoration hung from her neck by a chain. Ellie thought it like a long and slender pair of scissors, the shut blades stored in an equally slender case with a clasp. But the finger holes of the handle were set too close. Too much like—

A syringe or a punch dagger? Whether it was a medical

devise or a weapon, Ellie wondered why it wasn't concealed. But speculation wasted her time. The fluidity of their world could give her the shape; she just had no clue as to the purpose. Unless she asked the woman or touched the object herself, there was no point in guessing.

And she smells funny, Ellie thought. *The way them Catholic churches do. Except with roses in 'em.*

The woman took a step and Ellie stood up.

"Ellie?" Elvie cried.

—

Elvie's favourite object in the British Museum was a copy of the marble known as the *Aphrodite of Rhodes.*

Ellie called the *Aphrodite* Elvie's nymph, and perhaps she was that, a kneeling Venus turned as if alerted to someone watching her bathe, her arms raised to wring water from her long and wavy hair. She was small and placed on a pedestal tall enough for Elvie to meet her, nose to tiny nose. The *Aphrodite*'s face was quite worn away, but Elvie loved the roughness and the imperfect surfaces, which seemed to speak of longtime survival in the face of nature, time, and events of man. The *Aphrodite* had endured much and was still beautiful.

Elvie rested her head against the *Aphrodite* and embraced her little shoulders. She'd attempted to make a clay copy of her at home, and she was working on her fifth variation, finding that her shapes often developed into explorations deviating from the initial inspiration. Her *Aphrodites* seemed more about what she sensed when touching the body of the original rather than exercises at exact duplication, and she revelled in those discoveries. Some of her fellow boarders seemed to understand what she was attempting; their sighted housekeeper, Mrs Darby, merely called her clays "queer."

Elvie raised her arm and with a smile of anticipation, slowly brushed her wool sleeve against the stone of the *Aphrodite*'s body, from her breast to the smooth rise of her abdomen and down to the curve of her tensed thigh. She listened to the touch.

Shhhhhush. The soft sound sent a gentle tingle along her scalp and down her neck, thrilling her. Elvie found that she was singular in her physical response to certain, mundane sounds. Her fellow blind did not react so. The aural repetition of paper rustling, pens scratching, and stone being brushed graced her with soothing pleasure, one that could lull her into a stupor. She gently brushed the *Aphrodite* again, following the curves of her body down, and drew out the contact.

Shhhhhhhushh.

The tingles cascaded down her spine. Elvie shuddered, delighted, and her eyelids fluttered.

Shhhht . . ..

She stilled. She had not made that sound.

It came from behind her.

Shhhhhhh . . ..

Fabric; on stone. Someone else's sleeve. And then Elvie realised—

The scent of roses had not faded.

Shhhhhhhhhhuush.

Tingles radiated from her scalp and down her neck from a brushing of cloth made perfectly against stone. Elvie breathed the scent of pungent roses and shuddered.

This person knows, she thought, the thrill running down her back. *She knows the sound of stone.*

A woman's step lightly fell in her direction.

Elvie started. She was not ready to meet this person.

"Ellie?" she called nervously.

"What is it, Elvie?" Ellie said lightly, her voice suddenly next to her. Elvie put her hand out and contacted Ellie's body, tense beneath her palm. "You startled by another broken cucumber?"

"No, I—Ellie, is someone else here?"

Ellie did not answer, but Elvie suspected her pause was due to taking in, with her unique senses, the measure of the entire room.

"Ellie?" Elvie couldn't be certain, but she thought Ellie seemed surprised.

"Yes, Elvie, there was someone. Though that person's no longer present. Humph."

"Ellie, is something the matter?"

"Oh, nothing's the matter now, Elvie. Though I should step out. Just to feel about. The room will be entirely empty but fer you 'n the marbles. Will you be content to remain?"

"I will be, Ellie. I won't move an inch."

"There's a good girl. I'll just be a moment."

Elvie listened as Ellie departed swiftly. She'd known her to move thus only if Ellie thought something needed her especial attention immediately. Elvie shivered and hugged the *Aphrodite*.

"Oh, I hope there's nothing the matter," Elvie said to herself. "I may have reacted poorly."

Because the woman—well, why did she believe it was a woman? It was not beyond reason that a man, and quite a singular one, would favour such a fragrance.

No; Elvie was certain it was a woman, and one whose approach had flustered her. If she had handled the situation with better grace, she might have had someone new to speak to and Ellie might still be present rather than investigating.

"Ellie?" Elvie called. It was not like Ellie to leave her alone for very long.

The rose scent lingered. If she followed it, she might know where the woman had previously stood—and perhaps what sculpture she'd made that perfect sound upon. Elvie wouldn't mind replicating the sensation. She turned from the *Aphrodite* and felt her way, recalling the nearness of the sound. Her hands encountered the broad face of a smooth, circular column. She couldn't be certain, but it seemed the same spot from which she'd heard the custodian's heavy breathing on her last visit. The fragrance was strong there. Elvie felt her way around.

"Oh!" Her hand encountered another hand. Of stone, yet warm. It was a male hand that led to a chiseled cuff, sleeve, and—the marble was of a man in modern clothes. She could feel the seams in his waistcoat, the precise shaping of the links in the watch chain. All of the smooth surfaces she touched seemed warm. She raised her hands, and her fingers found the face. She traced it and discovered a chiselled moustache. The hairs were delicately formed, and she was astonished by the level of craftsmanship that could create such a likeness to true hairs. She felt the statue's lips, which were parted.

"Haaaaaa . . .. " the statue said. Warm breath blew against her fingertips.

Elvie screamed.

The monocled woman stepped back through the doorway and watched as Elvie fled from the marble man. She drew the metal syringe from the casing hanging from her chain, the long needle gleaming in the room's light. Elvie bumped, stumbled, and sobbed her oblivious way towards her, her hands frantic and reaching for each statue. The woman ran swiftly around and reached the marble man's side. She sank the needle into his neck just as Elvie found the entrance, calling for help.

CHAPTER TWO

Ellie had wanted a word with the monocled woman. When she exited Room 84, her quarry stood at the end of the hall and at Ellie's approach, stepped aside into a small room. Ellie followed, only for the doors to slide shut right as the woman slipped by her and back into the hall. Before Ellie could turn, the room moved; she was trapped in an ascension room, and one that ascended all the way to the roof. Having never ridden in such a contraption and being unable to discern the labelled buttons, Ellie exited, sought the stairs, and ran back down. To her relief, she found Elvie in emotional argument with museum staff, insisting upon an extraordinary story.

"He breathed on me, I tell you!" Elvie cried. "And he was made of stone!"

Ellie took pause at that. But she knew Elvie's senses; they were literal and true, even when fallen prey to an elaborate hoodwinking. The custodian, whom Elvie insisted had been a statue, was then very alive, though somehow having fainted. Ellie gave the revived custodian a solid knock despite already knowing that he was indeed, flesh.

However, Elvie remained adamant about what had

happened, and Ellie felt remiss in protecting her from the attentions of strange women or from custodians putting on foolish jests. She gave the man more knocks and a few threats regarding tricking blind girls and was only placated by his flustered superior's assurance that the man would lose his position at last.

"Well, Elvie, yer at least rid of the pest," she said during the carriage ride back to Southwark and the Institute of the Blind. "But I am sorry for leavin' you alone at that man's mercy. I'll return yer fee, if you like."

"No, Ellie, I," Elvie said and then sighed. She sat closer, and all Ellie could do was pat her hand.

"Turned into a statue? Elvie, you were surrounded by statues; that's the silliest mistake you could make!" Sarah said.

Back home at the Institute of the Blind, sitting with her fellow boarders in the drawing room, Elvie was having less luck convincing them of what happened than with Ellie. She clutched her knitting needles in frustration.

"I know what I felt, Sarah! It was a modern man of marble, his clothes, his face, his hand—all of him, carved of stone! And when I touched his lips, he gave a breath, a last sound!"

The room fell silent, as if all present held their own breaths at the thought.

"It was horrible," she said.

The others laughed.

"Oh, 'orrible, certainly!" Alan teased.

"Now that's enough, Alan," Mrs Darby, their sighted housekeeper, said. "You can make merry, but Elvie's had quite the adventure at the museum, and from a male pest

playing awful tricks, at that. You all would have had the
same fright yourself, had you been there!"

"I would 'ave *popped* 'im one for such a scare," Alan
declared, emphasising his words with, Elvie assumed, some
gesture in the air for punching. None of the Institute's
boarders would have known how to "pop" anything if not
for Ellie, who had showed them how. Such lessons in using
their bodies had given them all a little more confidence.

The doorknocker sounded.

"Don't answer it!" Mrs Darby cried before the boarders
could call out "haloo". "I'll see who's there." Elvie heard her
breathe as she moved her large form for the entryway and
its door. "It must be another journalist. Elvie, do you still —"

"Do I still not want to talk to any of them? Yes, Mrs Darby.
They're certain to make me sound like a fool in their papers."
She rose, keeping her needles close to her body should she
walk into one of her fellow boarders. "I'm walking now. Up
to my room. You may all continue laughing once I'm gone."

"Well, we can't know you're gone unless you tell us,
Elvie," Sarah said, then snickered.

"Oh, you'll know, Sarah, when I've tossed your other
pair of shoes down the stairs," Elvie said, and the others
laughed again. Mrs Darby conversed with someone at the
door while Elvie felt her way out of the drawing room and
for the staircase. The others talked, excited, dwelling on
her museum adventure. The lives of the blind tended to be
dull, often spent in earnest industry to prove their worth to
society, especially if they were supported by its charity. But
at the Institute, the rules were more lenient than the strict
and publicly funded Blind School, located a few buildings
away. The Institute's boarders could exercise independence,
coming and going as they pleased, as long as they paid for

their board and amenities. Adventures like the ones Ellie and Elvie had often enlivened the after-dinner discussions.

Elvie liked that she would still have a home at the Institute after reaching thirty years of age, whereas the Blind School would have turned her out. And she welcomed the blind children boarded there who were too young for acceptance at the Blind School, for then she had students to teach. She had had enucleation surgery at a very tender age, and the blind world was all Elvie had ever known. Until she was old enough to attend the Blind School, she'd been nothing but a helpless, housebound cripple, much as she appreciated her parents' love and care. And once they had passed away and her brother allowed the awarding of her allowance, Elvie wasted no time in applying for a room at the Institute. She wanted to be a functioning, independent woman, free to pursue her passions, especially in sculpting.

In her room, she touched each of her clays sitting on the shelf until she reached the windows and the setting sun's warmth. "Light" meant day and the presence of the very, very faraway celestial object (as explained to her) that was the sun. During such time, being awake and industrious was acceptable. "Dark" meant no warmth and signified night, the time of rest and slumber. But like many of her fellow boarders who had no need for illumination, Elvie often remained awake to knit stockings, read, or write, just as Sarah made baskets and Alan fashioned rugs. Elvie lived comfortably due to her allowance and teaching, but all residents supplemented payment for their board by selling the products of their skill and labour. Elvie took a seat by the window, feeling the fading sun, and resumed knitting. Despite having come home, eaten, and conversed, safe in the company of friends, she still felt the remnants of her scare at the museum.

"That awful man," she said. "Did he trick me, really?"

All she'd wanted was to trace the rose scent of her observer, and somehow, the custodian had slipped in without her marking his entrance (though she could not think how), and then played a statue for her benefit. Perhaps what Ellie had pointed out during the ride back home was true: he'd seen that she liked touching statues and thus rendered himself one, through some remarkable duplicity, just to entice her touch.

Elvie shuddered at the thought and put her knitting down.

"Wicked man," she muttered and rubbed at the pressure forming between her eye sockets. She went to her drawers to prepare a headache powder.

"Elvie?" Mrs Darby called as Elvie gulped down bitter powders and water. She heard the housekeeper lumber down the hallway.

I hope a journalist didn't pay her for permission to come up, Elvie thought, peeved, but she detected no additional steps. Mrs Darby's body brushed the frame of her open doorway.

"You've a letter, Elvie! Just brought by special post, and it's not from your brother. And what fine paper it is. The sender is a 'Lady Thanatou.' Elvie, I don't recall you mentioning having a lady for an acquaintance."

"The name sounds Greek, Mrs Darby," Elvie said, astonished, and held out her hands for the letter. "And I—I know no such person. Where is it from?"

When Mrs Darby answered, "Brompton,"which she explained was a hamlet situated in South Kensington and only six miles from Southwark, Elvie was stymied. The heavy paper of the envelope did feel of very high quality in her hands, just as Mrs Darby said. And it also smelled like—

Elvie put the envelope to her nose and inhaled. There was the touch of roses.

"Shall I read it for you, Elvie? I've my letter opener."

"Please, Mrs Darby." She handed back the letter. Mrs Darby set something heavy down—Elvie smelled that it was the oil lamp she carried, as the blind did not light their rooms—and ran her opener with a smooth *shrik* against the envelope. She unfolded the paper within.

"Oh! Well, Elvie, Lady Thanatou must be blind, for the letter is all in braille. And, and there's an additional card. It looks like an invitation."

"And that too is in braille?" Elvie felt the items returned to her hands. She ran her fingers along the dots of the card. She read aloud:

> Lady Thanatou
> cordially invites
> Miss Elvie Chaisty
> to join fellow artists
> in her Marble Garden
> for *Haphê*
> An appreciation of her latest works by touch.

"A marble garden? Oh my, I've been invited to something wonderful!" Elvie exclaimed. She ran her fingers over more dots. "And the event is for tomorrow!"

"What's that mean, Elvie, 'haphê'?" Mrs Darby asked.

"I know little Greek, as such lessons have yet to be coded into braille, but it sounds very much like the word *haptikos*, which means 'touch.' Mrs Darby, won't you find Ellie for me if she's not in her room?"

"I think she's still out escorting, Elvie—"

"Just look for her, please." She reached for Mrs Darby and urged her from her room. "I want her to take me to this notable gathering, and perhaps she'll know the address."

She shut her door on Mrs Darby and her protests and then put the letter to her nose. She inhaled.

"It's you, then," she whispered. "Now, who are you?" She ran her fingers along the raised dots of the letter.

Dear Miss Elvie Chaisty
You with the Aphrodite of Rhodes
I your witness intruded and must ask your forgiveness
I hope we could meet again and I may make amends
Yours Lady Thanatou

"How carefully this letter has been punched," Elvie said, "in the manner of the newly blind, with a hand unfamiliar with our braille's coding. Yet she is sighted, for she knew what marble I was with at the museum." She touched the embossed dots. "And she—or the one she dictated this to, chose to use no punctuation, lest they accidentally alter the purpose of the sentences." She raised the paper to her nose again. "No, she did not dictate this but punched the letter herself."

She read the invitation, and then the letter again. It was presumptuous to write such a letter to her without formal introduction, but Lady Thanatou had laid that course of impropriety when she'd brushed stone for Elvie's ears only. Respectability warred with curiosity, the nervous fluttering of her stomach, and a little with her pride, for she was terribly flattered that a lady should apologise to a common woman like herself. It made her regret even more the missed encounter at the museum.

"And had we met, that awful man might not have played his trick on me. Who are you, that understands the sound of stone and wears so glorious a fragrance? Rich and deep, hinting of mysteries and lineage." She rose with the letter held to her. "I shall know tomorrow, won't I? Until then, keep your secrets."

The next morning, Ellie rode in a hackney carriage with her client, the suffragette spokeswoman Mrs Husher-King, and thought about the monocled woman from the museum. Mrs Husher-King read aloud from the *Times*, relating the museum incident as reported by the journalist Helia Skycourt.

"'Clyde Barlew insisted that he'd played no such trick on the hapless Miss Chaisty but was the victim of a malevolence,'" she read, "'one cast by a mysterious, masked woman who looked upon him with a single eye.

"'It was a dreadful look!' he cried. 'So awful! It was a stare by the Queen of Hell!'"

Ellie snorted.

"'Mr Barlew then described his conversion into 'solid stone' as thus: transfixed, he was trapped in inescapable abeyance. He felt himself rigid, then rooted, and in such paralysis, his eyesight fled, his hearing reduced to a shallow roaring, and his breath grew scant. He perceived himself brushed upon, and then touched by delicate, inquisitive hands, to which he sought to utter a final, breathy plea.'"

"Recreant! I should 'ave given 'im something to plead about," Ellie muttered.

"And it goes on to describe his lament from losing his position, all the while professing his innocence." Mrs

Husher-King folded the newspaper closed and placed it with finality on her lap. She removed her pincer spectacles and looked at Ellie. Ellie could not discern a "look," but Mrs Husher-King's life-fire gave the soft intensity of kind intention. "I hope you don't blame yourself, Ellie. He seems a most devious character. One who even engaged an accomplice to distract you."

"At least an end's been put to 'is bamboozling, but now I know not to underestimate men who play at half-wits, Mrs Husher-King," Ellie said. Their carriage stopped, and Ellie accompanied her client out and for the Bethnal Green Working Girls Club at which Mrs Husher-King was engaged to speak.

But even as Ellie stifled yawns while listening to Mrs Husher-King address rapt worker girls, she thought again on the monocled woman, knowing that such a being as she had sensed would never give a lowly man like the custodian her attention, much less her compliance in a deceit. And that thought made Ellie uneasy.

By late morning she was back on the Institute grounds and, sensing no journalists to chase off, popped into the scullery entrance to request a cup of tea. There she found peg-legged Sgt Trilby, in his frayed long coat, engaged in earnest conversation with Mrs Darby. The old veteran was a frequent visitor of the Institute, especially for the cup and biscuit he could request at the scullery door, ever since he'd saved a despondent, newly blind boarder from ending his life at Blackfriars Bridge.

"Well, Sgt Trilby, what did she intend on the bridge? Except what desperate women do, who go when none can see their intentions!" Mrs Darby exclaimed.

"'Ave you saved another poor soul from a drownin', Sgt

Trilby?" Ellie enquired.

"Miss Hench!" He turned to her, his expression seemingly confounded. "Lord knows! Except that something did happen, same as I read happened to Miss Chaisty! For I saw it, yesterday evening. A young woman on the bridge turned to stone!"

Ellie neared. Trilby was known to drink, and right then he smelled as though he had been. She knew best if a person was telling the truth by their life-glows. When people desired to deceive, so did their light-fires, dimming and contracting. Trilby's shown bright like one desiring to reach those around him with his words.

Yet as with Elvie, Ellie thought, a duping performed on an old man could seem like truth to him.

"This 'appened on Blackfriars Bridge, where you do yer souvenir photography, Sgt Trilby?" Ellie said. "Yer not here to coax some coin from enquiring journalists, are you?"

"The thought is furthest from my mind," Trilby protested. "With the girl of stone gone, no one has reason to believe me!"

"Well, get on with it, Trilby, I'm still waiting for the rest," Mrs Darby said.

"As I've said, Mrs Darby, the girl is gone. But she was there, I tell you, and she turned to stone!"

"'Ow was this done, Sgt Trilby?" Ellie asked.

"A girl." Trilby gestured as if the girl were before them. "Came to stand at the parapet as many do, perhaps to contemplate the waters, the sunset, or St Paul's. I approached, thinking she might like a souvenir photograph of herself. But a carriage came between us and stopped. Then it pulled away. I neared . . . ."

Ellie watched as the planes of Trilby's face slackened and

his eyes widened. He ran a hand over his face as if to wipe his expression of horror away. "There she still stood, but one foot off the ground as if to lift herself over. And she looked behind, her face—oh! Such a look on her face!"

"What sort of look, Sgt Trilby?" Ellie said.

"It was a look all drained of colour! But it wasn't paleness, no! She just wasn't flesh, she—she was stone!"

"But Trilby," Mrs Darby said. "You said the girl was no longer there after you'd gone for help. Can a statue walk off?"

"I know what I saw! For I knew that look. I'd seen it in battle, that gaze of terror, fixated, as if staring upon *terrible* angels. For what the men saw was the bayonet or cannonball that came for them! And I touched her, if only to prove that it could not be so. I . . . ." He looked at his hand, which trembled. "She breathed on me! It wasn't the wind! I saw the puff made white by our night air, issued from her marble lips. The breath was *warm*."

"Sgt Trilby," Mrs Darby said in concern as the old veteran covered his face. She rose to fetch him tea. Ellie gave him a reassuring pat on the back.

"Oh!" Trilby exclaimed from the smack.

"Be comforted, Sgt Trilby, that like the museum custodian, that poor girl must 'ave recovered from 'er 'orrible condition, and is right this minute drinkin' 'er tea. As Mrs Darby said, a statue could not walk away." She turned for the door leading into the house.

"Miss Hench!" Trilby called. "Assure Miss Chaisty that she witnessed the truth!"

"Oh, I shall, Sgt Trilby," Ellie said.

Even with her back turned, she read in the fluid-flow how he pressed his hands in prayer.

"So this breath you felt, Elvie, it came from the statue's lips?" Ellie said. She was seated in Elvie's room while her friend worked on a small clay figure, yet another of her nymphlike *Aphrodites*.

"My fingers were right on those lips, for I was touching his moustache," Elvie said. "The breath was warm, Ellie."

"Humph."

"What a cruel trick to play on me. And with poor Trilby— might it have been drink and his own perceptions deceiving him? But I can't fathom how all this can happen if it were *not* illusion; first the custodian and then this girl you speak of. Perhaps it's a new paralysing disease?"

"If it were, you'll be arthritic soon, Elvie," Ellie said.

"You'd know, Ellie. You'd be able to sense such condition in me."

"True. It would be in yer life-glow. Not a bit of you is stiffening."

"Good. Then you can take me to this wonderful artistic event I've the honour of being invited to." Elvie moved around her clay, the shape of which seemed like a very simple, curvaceous feminine form to Ellie's perceptions, and dabbed a bit more clay on the bulblike head.

"Much as I like fêtes fer the food and well-bathed men, I need to speak to someone 'bout—well, something that concerns me, Elvie. And this someone has a 'ead for strange things."

"Ellie, you can't leave, I need you to chaperone me! I'll— I'll have to go without you if you won't stay."

"Now, Elvie, 'aven't you thought more on why yer invited? Isn't it peculiar?"

"Of course it's peculiar. Which makes me want to go

even more." Elvie ran her fingers along the sides of the clay. "I lost my chance to speak to the rose-scented woman at the museum, and I regret my shyness. Her letter is most surprising and makes me question why I've—well, it seems like she's an admirer. And I can't understand why."

"Oh, she's an admirer, that's certain," Ellie said. "I'd laugh at the notion if this woman weren't so queer."

"How queer? And what do you mean, you'd laugh?"

"Wait 'til she finds out yer the perverse one. 'Oh, might I touch your breasts? I only want to know if they're like mine!'" Ellie mocked in a squeaky falsetto.

"I do not sound like that!" Elvie said, her tone indignant.

"You are not to go out," Ellie said. "Not 'til I tend to some things. If she's set on makin' yer acquaintance, there will be ample time for 'er to find something else to invite you to. For now, stay and play with your clays, do you 'ear me, Elvie?"

"I'm a grown woman and you're not my mother!"

"I'm ten years yer elder and will box those grown ears if you don't heed me," Ellie said.

"Very well," Elvie answered, her tone sullen. "Promise me you'll return very soon? Perhaps there will still be time for you to take me to this event."

"Certainly," Ellie said.

———

Ellie emerged from the underground rail in Westminster twenty minutes later, queried within the Royal Aquarium, boarded an omnibus, then hopped off at a stop in Chelsea. A newsboy pointed to the fenced-off site she wanted, surrounded by storied business buildings.

"The Quaker versus the Quake Maker? Right in there,

Miss!"

She followed the fence, found a loosened board beneath a peeled-back, pasted bill, and stepped through the opening to stand at the rim of a vast excavation pit. At the very bottom and amidst the rubble of demolished foundations, two formidably sized supernatural agents of HRH's Secret Commission stood frozen in the bright sunlight, locked in a wrestlers' embrace.

Artifice, artificial ghost and strongwoman, had stripped down to her corset, chemise, and skirts, while Atlas the Quake Maker was clad in only his trousers and boots, his chest hair running like an arrow down to his navel. Art gripped his waistband and Atlas, the bottoms of her corset. Their muscular arms flexed, and their legs braced as they leaned into each other, refusing to be lifted. Ellie narrowed her focus upon the tense swells of Atlas's buttocks.

"Now those are shapes to remark upon," she said.

The pit was a perfect setting for such titans to engage in combative recreation, ensuring no damage to the rest of London. Spectators were spread all about the pit or upon rubble, as if viewing a sedate cricket match. Parasols dotted the levels, and Ellie noted distant faces watching from the windows of the buildings overlooking the area. She studied the fluid world, searching for certain distinct figures, and found them with the combatants below. One was a lean fellow with large hands and jaunty bowler, the other was a human skull in top hat, seated on a block of concrete. Mr Hands of Thunder, partner to Atlas, and Jim Dastard, animated skull and partner to Art, smoked cigarettes and shouted encouragement. Farther up the pit sat a petite, pretty figure beneath a small parasol. The fluid world gave back the planes of her composed face; Manon, a woman-in-residence at the private club, the Vesta, and also companion to Art. Ellie didn't doubt that beneath her calm, receptive facade, the young woman was bored stiff.

If Ellie cast her search wider, she might soon mark the trim, austere lines of Art's benefactress, Lady Helene Skycourt, observing the match from a well-obscured (at least to sighted people) location. And perhaps by her side would be her man, the wiry and square-shouldered Gurkha, Ganju Rana. But Ellie needed to find one of Art's circle in particular. That one shone like a malignant pestilence in an otherwise healthy fluid-flow. And many might consider the madwoman and journalist, Helia Skycourt, twin sister to Helene, just such a malignancy.

Ellie progressed around the pit to where Helia sat, high above the others, her hands clasping a handheld typing devise to her chest as she watched below. Her smart cavalier hat lent her an attractive profile, and she leaned with the entranced attention of a smitten schoolgirl. The half-mask she wore faced Ellie, but Ellie could sense right through the bewitched leather to the eldritch infection Helia secretly bore.

Ellie picked her way around the earth and rubble and reached Helia, who turned her head and smiled in greeting.

"I feel slighted, Helia. You neglected to interview me fer yer museum story," Ellie hailed.

"But Ellie, you don't like to be in the papers."

"True. And I still don't."

The grapplers moved, Atlas driving Art back. She dug her heels in and furrowed earth until Atlas could budge her no more. She remained as immobile as granite.

The men murmured in excitement, and the ladies laid down their telescopes and opera glasses to clap. Below Helia and Ellie, a seated man remarked to another.

"Such power harnessed could run our pumping stations," he said. "Are you certain you want to keep your wager on the ghost?"

"I do!" his companion exclaimed.

Ellie knocked about with her stick though she already knew what of the earth was sound, and then sat down next to Helia. "Once, I visited the seaside," she said. "The ocean, it's quite a sensation, one I barely can give the entirety of my comprehension. I also witnessed a lighthouse, and I couldn't discern its beam as some tried to describe it, but I knew its 'eart, its fiery beacon." She pointed with her stick to the combatants below. "There grapple two big beacons; their presence so strong, I felt it through the fencing."

Helia smiled and turned back to watch the two. "Art has met a fellow agent from whom she needn't withhold the whole of her strength. She is terribly happy."

"I don't know why you had 'er brought back a Quaker still, Helia. I understand she was that tall and broad before 'er death, yet it was no 'elp in savin' 'er from death, thanks to 'er peaceful nature. You could 'ave had the Quaker part subtracted from the alchemy of 'er resurrection. When we fought, she let me break 'er nose when she could have easily knocked me dead."

"But that is her, Ellie. It is Art," Helia said. "I would never deny her that aspect."

"We have in Art a powerful thing constrained, that's certain." Ellie scratched her nose. "I may have another such creature on me 'ands. Constraining 'erself."

"How do you mean, Ellie?"

Male voices rose, crying, "Ho! Ho! Ho!" as Atlas lifted Art's body until she stood on tiptoe. Art hugged Atlas more and slowly compressed, bringing her heels back down. She heaved Atlas up in turn.

"Oh! Grab hold!" Helia said.

Boom!

Atlas brought his feet back to earth in a rising cloud of dust, averting Art's throw. The ground quaked from his impact, and bits of mortar and loosened dirt tumbled down the sides of the pit. A few people slid as earth gave way, and Ellie braced herself with her stick. A sharp thunderclap followed as Mr Hands of Thunder slapped his palms together in satisfaction. Jim shouted and erupted into a brief, hot blaze.

"I'm no detective, Helia," Ellie said as the spectators righted themselves and Atlas and Art renewed their deadlock. "I simply hit things. And my stick's of little consequence to certain beings."

"Tell me your trouble," Helia said.

———

Ellie waited while Helia made her careful way down the pit to Manon then back up again, and noted with stern approval that Art did not allow sight of Helia to distract her. If Art had a weakness (besides being a Quaker), it was in her "skirts-chasing," as Jim would call it, and nothing drew her gaze more than the women she had affection for.

"I've given my message to Manon. We may depart," Helia said when she reached Ellie's side. Ellie remained still, concentrating her focus right down to the threads in the taut seat of Atlas's trousers. Should Art pull up again, the straining cloth could split at any minute.

"Ellie?" Helia said.

"Just thinkin' on Christmas dinner. Off we go." She turned with Helia and chose their path out of the pit.

"Now, Ellie, the news of this monocled woman and her marble-garden event is quite interesting," Helia said as she followed. "Miss Chaisty should perhaps not attend, due to the coincidence of people turning into statues."

Ellie snorted. "Bosh. That Trilby tipples, I told you. He thought he saw the girl on Blackfriars Bridge in a manner marble-like. The night's obscurities can hoodwink you sighted lot. Did y'visit the Institute yesterday and speak to Elvie?"

"I tried, but the housekeeper turned me away."

"Y'didn't offer enough coin, Helia."

"Really, I hadn't time. There was another matter more pressing needing attention."

"Yer speakin' of the museum custodian?"

Ellie did not have to turn around to know that Helia scowled, the expression a cold spot in the life-glow of her face. "Museum rapist is more like it. During the interview, I knew. And no, I haven't proof for that assumption."

The eldritch presence behind Helia's half-mask bloomed and stretched, casting tendrils into the world-fluid. Ellie shrugged off her shudder.

"The knowledge of yer nose is proof enough for me," she said casually, her senses measuring the slow withdrawal of the creature into Helia's life-glow. Soon it would disappear, gone back to sleep again. "So you believe that pismire's story?"

"I do. I think he spoke the truth. Something turned him to stone."

They reached the loosened fence board and exited, the earth shuddering once more. Behind them, men shouted in surprise and women gasped in astonishment, and Ellie thought the women did so with some glee. She imagined split trousers, sighed, and waved for a hackney carriage.

"Helia, I 'ave asked you to investigate a bamboozlin',
especially where a most uncommon woman is concerned,
or not concerned, just to ease my mind 'bout Elvie and her
queer lady, and you talk of people becoming rocks. Explain
it, then."

"Of course, Ellie. This was the manner of his paralysis: he
looked upon an eye too dreadful to behold."

"That part was read to me from yer story. Do you mean a
single eye, Helia?"

"Yes, Ellie. He looked upon an Evil Eye."

"An evil regard that struck 'im immobile." Ellie pondered
as a carriage neared. "I wonder what that's like. I've never
sensed a shape that could so confound me."

"The look did more than that. The custodian did not
know it, but he was speaking of a face once mounted on
ancient shields. A powerful prophylactic to attract and baffle
the angry gaze. And in so doing, it paralyses the onlooker,
permanently. How fortunate for your friend that this power
worked to her favour, saving her from potential outrage."

"First an eye, now a face? Did I miss a portion of this
conversation?" Ellie said. The carriage driver halted his
horse and worked the lever to swing the door open.

"I apologise, dear. It's simple, really," Helia said as Ellie
boarded. "He looked upon an eye that terrified, then turned
him to stone. I believe what he witnessed was the eye
belonging to the face of the Gorgon."

⁓

After Helia had given the driver an address and she and
Ellie settled in the carriage, Helia related the myth of the
Gorgon.

"And when Athena discovered that Poseidon had outraged golden-haired Medusa in her temple, she transformed the poor girl, and her sisters who stood in defence of her, into creatures of serpent hair and frightening visage, at which sight the beholder was rendered to stone. According to Hesiod, the two older sisters, Stheno the Mighty and Euryale the Far Springer, were immortal, but Medusa the Queen was not, and was slain by the hero Perseus, who took her head and with it, transformed his enemies to stone."

"So . . . this 'ead did the deed by starin' at folks?"

"I would say their paralysis was rendered due to her singular looks."

"Then why isn't the custodian stone now, Helia? Or the girl on the bridge?"

"That, we must find out."

Stuff and nonsense, Ellie thought. "Very well; this Gorgon. Yer speaking of an 'orrible mask shown the custodian." She thought of the monocled woman but could not recall her mask as being the least bit disconcerting. Except for, perhaps, it being a mask.

"No, Ellie, I speak of a face. A terrifying face."

"She 'eld up a funny visage, then."

"No, Ellie, it was a woman's face. The woman you want investigated. If only to discern why she is quite interested in your friend."

"Hm. Well, if she removed 'er mask and shown 'erself so disfigured, I will assume for that custodian's sake that he's a silly one to be so frightened. Must have been a very funny visage."

"He did not witness a funny visage," Helia said. "He merely saw her eye. And because of that, I believe she has the power of which I spoke."

"Hm," Ellie said again. The carriage rolled and Helia bumped into her. Instead of fiddling with her handheld typing devise, she was scribbling in her notebook.

"A most dreadful eye," Helia added, still scribbling. "Belonging to a terrifying face."

You would know somethin' 'bout that, Miss Skycourt, Ellie thought. *Though I'd never sensed its face in yer face—if that crawly infection y'have has one.* She pulled out her pocket watch and felt the braille dots. "Are we off to see the woman possessing this eye, then? The monocled woman who, in yer story, is supposed to be beheaded?"

Helia laughed and kicked her feet in obvious glee. "Oh, what a mystery! Now we'll learn what of the myths might be tosh. Her being mortal, for one. We're not visiting your monocled woman just yet. There's a girl we must meet, Dolly Teegan, daughter of the wealthy American, Tiberius Teegan. Her maid read the museum story and wrote me a swift letter in confidence, claiming her mistress plans to turn herself into stone."

"How interestin'. Now this paralysis has become the fashion of the hoity-toits."

"Perhaps," Helia said, "except the maid believes her mistress does not want to return, but remain dead."

CHAPTER THREE

Elvie paused in work on her latest *Aphrodite* and pulled out her pocket watch. She popped the lid open, felt the braille dots upon the crystal face, smiled, shut the case, and put the watch away. Room tidied, braille classes taught, and lunch more or less eaten (for she felt too nervous), there was still time to work a little more before leaving for the marble-garden event.

And then I meet you at last, she thought, thinking on the monocled woman Ellie had described. She had sounded as tall as Ellie—which, compared to Elvie, was quite tall— well-formed and memorable of figure and appearance, wearing both metal mask and a snood.

"What a mystery you are," Elvie mused. She recalled the rose fragrance again, and it reminded her of a carol. She sang:

Frankincense to offer have I
Incense owns a Deity nigh

Prayer and praising, all girls raising
Worship Her, Goddess most high

O—*oh!*
Star of wonder, star of night
Star with royal beauty bright
Westward leading, still proceeding
Guide us to Thy perfect light

Myrrh is mine, its bitter perfume
Breathes of life of gathering gloom
Sorrowing, sighing, bleeding, dying
Sealed in the stone-cold tomb—

"Elvie!" she heard from her open door. "Have you gone daft? Why are you carolling?"

"Oh Sarah! You half-wit!" Elvie said. "How you startled me!"

Sarah laughed. "It's May, and you're carolling." Elvie heard her move away, then return. "Hold on, did you change the words again?"

"Sarah, go away," Elvie said loudly.

"You're a changeling, Elvie, that's what you are. A changeling needing baptism."

"And you're a *half-wit*." But Sarah was already moving down the hall, laughing again.

"Half-wit," Elvie muttered. She stopped work on her clay, feeling pressure grow in her head, and rubbed between her eyes. She went to her dresser to bathe her eye sockets and prepare another headache powder.

Medicine ingested and her eye sockets washed, she opened the top drawer of her dresser and searched for her glass, ocular prostheses. She possessed a pair of "Sympathetic Artificial Eyes," said to be the most perfect eyes invented and capable of moving about with one's own eyeballs—if Elvie still had her eyeballs. The oculist had assured her that the movement of her eye muscles would do. The prostheses had been an expensive purchase, and she'd never had an interest in pretending she'd true eyes, anyway. But she couldn't resist having them made, just to test if they lent her face that boasted naturalism and "lifelike" state. The glasses were modelled (she'd been told), after the captivating, sky-blue eyes of an English stage actress.

And if "sky-blue" might be like the captivating, lighthearted laugh she'd heard a woman give while playing with her baby in the park on a warm, supposedly sky-blue summer day, then that was what Elvie wanted to wear.

The moment she received the glass eyes from the oculist, she inserted them and visited London zoo, pretending she could stare at the caged animals and her fellow visitors. She even moved her eye muscles about; to the left, right, and up and down, feeling her glass eyes move accordingly. When she heard people's feet hurry away and children exclaim at her presence, she decided then that her "Sympathetic Eyes" were not achieving the effect of "sky-blue" allurement.

She stretched her right eye open and slipped in the glass. It seated itself against her flesh, and she grimaced. The fit was not perfect, and she'd known the glass to be comfortable in the past.

"If that Sarah has switched eyes with me again," she muttered.

She'd begrudgingly let Sarah try her "Sympathetic" right eye to impress a potential sweetheart. Sarah had lost her right eye to disease and relied on very poor monocular vision—

one too dim for her to be considered sighted. Prostheses were fitted to each client, yet Sarah had insisted that Elvie's eye fit her perfectly. Elvie popped in her left glass, which felt more comfortable. If Sarah had left Elvie her own inferior glass, she hoped the colours of the irises at least matched. Sarah had said she had blue eyes, but Mrs Darby had told Elvie that Sarah meant brown. Whatever "brown" was.

Elvie put on her spectacles and hat, located her invitation, and after patting herself all about to make certain she was presentable, found her willow stick. She sat down and waited.

After a while, she rose to find a book to read, but she was too nervous to concentrate on the braille. She pulled out her pocket watch, popped open the lid, and touched the dots marking the dial. Her heart sank at noting the time.

"Even with a fast hansom cab, we'll be too late. So rudely late. I'll never have my chance to go to this event."

The pricks of tears began.

"Elvie," she heard Mrs Darby call. Her heavy, slow steps sounded in the hall as she approached the doorway. "There's a very smart carriage arrived for you, Elvie. It's meant to take you to that artist's party you're invited to!"

"Mrs Darby?" Elvie said in surprise. She stood up, stick in hand. "Do you mean it's from my hostess—Lady Thanatou?"

At Mrs Darby's confirmation, Elvie nearly knocked her over, hurrying for the stairs. She descended as quickly as she could, Mrs Darby huffing and following.

"Mind the—children, don't come up, Elvie is coming down! Elvie, I don't know if I should let you leave. If you'd met the woman before—"

"Yes! Yes, I have, Mrs Darby. I'd met her. We—we just hadn't time to exchange names. Now we'll be properly introduced."

"Then you ought to have a chaperone—"

"Ellie will meet me there," Elvie said. "Tell her to go to the address if she should come here first. Oh, Mrs Darby, I will be safe and cared for, for isn't this an event given by a lady?"

"Well," Mrs Darby said, her tone uncertain. "Ah-hum. Those stories I read you lot about wicked toffs and ladies and—and their luring ways and such."

"Mrs Darby, pish! Those are penny stories."

"But Ellie says some of it's true, Elvie. She's been to their private clubs! And—and here you are, with this mysterious—"

"I'll be attending an artistic gathering to appreciate debuting marbles, Mrs Darby, not a vulgar private club. It's not so mysterious as that." Elvie stepped upon the landing where small hands touched her, attempting to reach for the bannister. She guided the hands to it and heard the children step up. She turned to face the drawing room.

"Here I come," Elvie called as she moved across the hall and through the drawing room for the entryway. Her sweeping cane encountered the chairs, tables, and settees she knew to be there. No one answered her call; the drawing room was empty. She touched the furniture until she made the turn for the door and sunlight fell on her reaching hand.

"The door's open, Elvie," Mrs Darby said. "It's wide open for you."

"Thank you, Mrs Darby. Expect me back by dinnertime. Here I come," she called again. She stepped out the doorway for her waiting carriage.

Ellie and Helia's carriage rolled down Upper Brook Street in Mayfair, surrounded by tall, terraced houses of a dignified air. Ellie loudly cleared her nose on her kerchief, then straightened her spectacles while Helia continued to scribble madly in her notebook. The carriage slowed before a home of five storeys bearing elegant, small balconies fenced with wrought iron. Sitting against the walk was a trim one-seater open-air electric buggy, steered by a tiller and set on a simple suspension between four large wheels. It appeared no bigger than a woman's tricycle, except that it was high and bore an electric battery and motor.

"A wee, horseless carriage," Ellie remarked.

"Oh, what a splendid racer," Helia said in admiration. "Perfect for one woman, light and fast."

Near the vehicle, a sinewy man with no hat stood with four rough-looking men in caps. They watched Ellie and Helia disembark from the carriage, then at a word from the hatless man, moved behind the walk's low, wrought-iron fence and trimmed hedge to descend for the scullery below.

"Not deliverymen," Helia said as the men disappeared.

"No," Ellie said. She approached the front door. "And the features of the hatless one. Italian?"

"I think more Greek, Ellie."

Ellie rapped on the door with her stick. After a while of knocking, an elderly butler answered, bent and balding, his eyes watery and sad. He stared blankly at the two.

"Good day," Helia said. She handed him her card. "I am Miss Skycourt and this is Miss Hench. We're here to see Miss Teegan on a matter of utmost importance."

"You are friends of Miss Teegan?" he said, his voice hoarse.

"Yes. Yes, we are friends. It is urgent we see her," Helia said.

"She invited you to . . . to *see* her." His eyes moistened more, and Ellie measured the liquid shapes on the surfaces of his orbs. "Yes, of course." He moved aside to let them in.

Helia and Ellie quickly entered.

"Might I enquire—her lady's maid, Mary?" Helia began as the butler led them down the hallway to the main staircase. He glanced back at her.

"Oh, Mary is . . . she can't right now. If you've need of anything—"

"No thank you, not right now," Helia said. She gave Ellie a look.

Ellie shrugged. Perhaps because the household belonged to an American, the butler had grown lax at maintaining appearances. They followed him up four flights of stairs, and Ellie thought it a conventional, hoity-toit home until they reached the fourth landing. Large sliding doors of metal lattice and ornate glass stood before them, wide open. Her sense of the fluid-world expanded to take in, behind those doors, a high-ceilinged conservatory with gallery, filled with towering palms and ferns. Marbles and antiquities sat on pedestals all about the tiled floor, and beyond the space was another set of veranda doors, opening to an outdoor balcony. A tall, distinguished-looking man stood within the conservatory, his back to them. The butler led Ellie and Helia inside, and Ellie noted the life-size, female marble, petite and delicate, that the man faced, placed before an elegant fountain.

The butler stopped.

"Mr Teegan," he said softly. "Two of Miss Dolly's friends to witness her."

When Tiberius Teegan ignored them, the butler stepped aside and gestured to where Teegan stood.

"Our miss," he said in a low voice.

But Ellie had her attention on another person present in the conservatory, one whose uncanny life-glow flared next to the far, spiral staircase leading up to the gallery.

The monocled woman turned, ascended the steps without a sound, then disappeared above.

"Oh, she is nimble," Ellie murmured. She stepped to pursue, then stopped. Four people were present on the conservatory floor, surrounded by palms and marbles, yet she sensed a fifth life-glow. She focused her awareness on where Teegan stood.

"Ellie?" Helia said. Ellie ignored her and approached him.

Teegan, with his strong shapes of forehead, nose, and chin that Ellie thought handsome, stood gazing at the marble before him. It was of a young woman no taller than his shoulder, dressed in a simple, classical Greek dress and her dangling curls bound up in pearls. Her hands were clasped at her breast, and she raised her expectant eyes as if awaiting a portentous arrival.

Ellie took in the whole of the statue, every plane and line, from the indentations of the nail beds to the delicately chiseled eyebrows above the wide, open eyes. In all of the stone, she witnessed a life-glow, so light it was a mere glimmer, similar to that of a flower in its final curling. The glimmer dimmed, and Ellie reached for Teegan's hand. She grabbed it and made him touch the statue's lips.

"Feel it. There's yer good-bye," she said in a rough voice.

"What?" he ejected, fingers trembling. His eyes widened in realisation and his face screwed up. He felt the lips more, then laid his head next to the statue's. He sobbed.

"Ellie," Helia said.

"Yes, Helia, this is Dolly Teegan," Ellie said.

———

Helia stared at Ellie standing next to the sobbing Teegan and was faintly aware of the butler departing for the door, suppressing his own grief. She stepped closer until she reached the conservatory's centre. She viewed the marble, a girl rendered lifelike. The girl's gaze was raised to the gallery, her face a state of calm touched, Helia felt, with wide-eyed rapture.

Yet she sensed another gaze, one right upon herself that chilled her to the bone. The masked side of her face itched and the eldritch infection within curled. Helia took a shuddering breath and turned to look up.

In the deep shadows of the gallery, she saw the shape of a still woman looking down, her monocle glinting. Helia turned to Teegan.

"Mr Teegan, if we hurry, we can bring your daughter back," she said. "What—"

But then the Greek man from the street stepped into the conservatory, smelling of nervous sweat. At the sight of Dolly Teegan's marble, his face darkened with anger. He pointed at Teegan.

"Teegan! I tried to help you, but you both still— Why did you do this?" he demanded.

"I did it for Dolly, Stavros, you fool," Teegan said, his voice hoarse. His tall frame remained bent over the marble. "Your idea of a trap—it no longer matters."

The other man laughed. "It is you who are the fool. You, with no understanding that the creature withheld her greatest power from you." His mouth twisted. "She has the gift of death, yes, *and*! And of life! She is a *pharmakon*!"

"Get out," Teegan said. "You make no sense, get out!"

"My men are on the stairs," Stavros said. "She will not leave here alive."

He approached, and Ellie stepped before Teegan, her long blackthorn in hand. Stavros halted, fists clenched.

"You and your daughter . . . you are nothing but her *pharmakos*," he imparted in derision. He noticed Helia and started.

"Another," he said, "with a mask." He turned and departed.

"Mr Teegan," Helia said with urgency. "We must—"

"No," he interrupted. "No." His voice cracked and he said no more.

Helia stood in surprise and uncertainty, while Ellie remained where she was, head cocked, and Helia knew she was marking the presence of the monocled woman above. Helia stepped around her to Teegan.

"Mr Teegan," she addressed softly. "I am Helia Skycourt. A journalist, but I assure you, I will write nothing regarding you and"—she looked towards the marble—"your daughter's chosen fate. Can you at least tell me more regarding the woman who did this?" She nearly gulped and tried not to look to the gallery, where she still felt the burning gaze. "For I am concerned for another young woman. Please tell us why this happened."

Teegan raised his head, eyes wet, and cupped the statue's face.

"Dolly had . . . she—a woman's ailment," he answered.

"Mr Teegan, we are women, you can tell us," Helia said.

"Just like her mother," he said. "Malignancies in her breast. Nothing could be done, and we were told there was little time left. She did not want to die like her mother did. So very ill, so . . . less her beautiful, wonderful self. I think

Dolly also saw what her mother's suffering did to me."

He heaved, and the shuddering sigh shook him. "I didn't agree to this solution," he said. "What father would? But then I had to, because she wanted it. She shared my love for all of this." He gestured to the other marbles. "Our antiquities. Our dedication—no, our *worship* of the ancient world. Somehow, after we met her—somehow, Dolly knew what that woman could do. And Dolly thought *this* her rightful fate. She didn't want me to suffer burying her in the ground."

He turned and gazed above.

"You saw her resolve," he cried up to the gallery. "'No more pain,' she had said. I can't ask you to bring her back."

The monocled woman's chin lowered, her eyepiece glinting. Teegan returned his gaze to Dolly.

"It would be selfish to ask her to come back," he softly cried.

Helia swallowed. "Mr Teegan . . . just one more question. Why did Stavros call you a *pharmakos*?"

He shook his head. "I don't know. Now, please."

Helia nodded. She touched Ellie, who followed as they left Teegan and the statue of Dolly behind for the other end of the conservatory. The balcony outside the veranda doors overlooked a garden. Each time she glanced over her shoulder at the gallery, the monocled woman stood there, cloaked in the shadows.

"Wot's this farm-a-cos, Helia?" Ellie asked.

"A *pharmakos* is an ancient Greek sacrifice, Ellie. A poor scapegoat's life given for some atonement. A city might perform this ritual by tossing a criminal or slave from a cliff. Or a cripple."

"Or a blind person. Is this wot they teach you hoity-toits

when you're learnin' Latin and such?"

"No," Helia said, her tone sober. "It's what I like to learn. What do you want to do now, Ellie?"

"I want words with 'er," Ellie said. "Just pleasantries, regardin' Elvie."

Helia nodded even as Ellie left and mounted the spiral staircase. But when Ellie stepped to the gallery above, Helia could no longer hear her footfall. She glanced up, seeing neither Ellie nor the monocled woman. Blinking, she scanned again, and the gallery appeared as empty as she had perceived it. She tried not to worry.

The butler looked into the conservatory, his aspect as lost as his employer's, and then withdrew. Stavros briefly glanced in with suspicion. Not once did Teegan move. He seemed a statue himself, and Helia understood his condition, remembering her nightlong vigil over Art's body in the Secret Commission. She looked at the graceful back of Dolly Teegan, thinking her marble so lifelike that in the right light, she might be mistaken for being alive again.

"Did you want control of your death?" she asked softly of the figure's back. "And when you found one with that power, did commanding her give you some measure of triumph?"

Helia's gaze dropped. "I know that feeling. I commanded a resurrection."

Something screamed behind her, the unearthly cry echoing in the conservatory. Helia's hands flew up, then she spun around, wondering at the same time why Teegan did not react. Before her on the balcony, a blue peacock stood, trailing magnificent, long, green tail feathers.

With a majestic shake it spread its plumes. A great fan of iridescent green eyes stared at Helia.

"Hera," Helia said, and a deep unease then nagged within

her. She smelled roses mixed with frankincense and turned. There stood the monocled woman.

Purple her sails, and so perfumed, Helia thought.

The woman wore a black velvet snood glittering with purple embroidery thread. Its band was tight to her powdered, white forehead and the sides of her soft oval face, the snugness of the band as severe as that of a starched wimple. Her round chin was white with a rouged, full-lipped mouth. And against the upper half of her face, concealing the nose, she wore a finely hammered gold half-mask, bearing no opening for the left eye. Instead, the blank surface was illustrated with the simple graphic of a kohl-lined eye and arched brow. Affixed to the right eyehole was a large protruding gold monocle. Helia stared at the thick lense and spied a brilliant blue eye staring back.

Helia touched her half-mask. The woman touched her own.

The baleful gaze fixed upon her. Were the woman to remove her glass, Helia did not doubt that the basilisk-blue of her glaring orb would be the last image she'd know. The woman held the edge of her mask.

"A warning." Helia's voice shook. "Though my curse has an insect's lifespan compared to yours, it has a frightening instinct for self-preservation."

The woman paused, the fix of her gaze intensifying. She dropped her hand, and Helia dropped hers. The woman turned, her odd pendant case with its syringe handle swaying on her bosom, and swept for the conservatory's spiral staircase. She ran up it with inhuman speed and in a blink, disappeared into the gallery again, her feet making no sound.

Men spoke urgently outside the conservatory, then

stampeded up the main staircase in the hallway for the gallery above. Before Helia could run for the spiral stairs, something rumbled and a metal gate slid open. She turned, seeking the source of the sound, but it was hidden behind tall, potted ferns. Ellie burst from their fronds.

"Up there!" Helia said, pointing to the gallery as men ran above. Helia spared Teegan a glance.

He continued staring at his daughter's marble, ignoring all while the peacock strutted. Ellie ran for the spiral staircase and Helia followed.

"Should she trick me a third time, I'll give up me stick," Ellie declared as they climbed. "This 'ouse has a secret ascension room. She sent me to the basement this time."

"Oh, Ellie! The same trick as at the museum? Please don't blame yourself. She's two thousand years old—a queen to we mere pawns."

"I still failed you, Helia, just like Elvie. Are you harmed?"

"No, but she gave me quite the fright. Truly, she possesses the apotropaic gaze, to paralyse we profaners."

"Mm-hm," Ellie said. Once in the gallery she walked quickly, her chin high and blackthorn at the ready.

"Ellie, did you notice her odd pendant?" Helia said, staying behind her.

"I did. Was it a dagger?"

"No, I believe it was a syringe."

Ellie turned into the open door of a guest bedchamber. She kept walking right for the windows and pointed with her stick to one that was pushed open. Helia heard scuffling outside.

"There she is. Five against 'er one," Ellie said. She jumped out the window while Helia scampered to follow.

CHAPTER FOUR

Elvie stood on the drive of the Institute of the Blind, her stick having found a vehicle waiting before her, and grinned broadly. A young woman greeted her from beside the vehicle.

"*Khaîre*, Miss Chaisty. I am Corrina, attendant to my Lady Thanatou, and I will accompany you on your journey to Old Brompton. Here also is Ahmet, footman of our household, who shall describe to you our journey, and Alexys, our driver."

"How do you do," Elvie said, liking Corrina's subdued, yet calm, warm tone. "I am both honoured and very delighted by the offer of this conveyance by Lady Thanatou." She held out her hand, but the woman's hand that met it did not shake it. Instead Corrina gently guided her to the side of the carriage, and Elvie, appreciating the opportunity, patted the polished wood.

"Our lady desires very much that you attend her marble-garden event," Corrina said. "Thank you, miss, for coming."

"May I infer from your names that you are Greek? Though you are servants, I am an independent, blind woman and don't often observe the ranks of our stations." A man's large, warm hand took her wandering one while Corrina held her right and guided her stick. They helped her board the carriage.

"You honour us, miss," Ahmet said, his voice rich and deep. "And you are correct; Corrina and Alexys are Greek while I am Turkish." Elvie settled against a leather-smelling stuffed seat and noted that his voice sounded above her, as if he stood on a platform behind her seat.

"Why, this is an open-air vehicle!" she exclaimed, feeling the sun on her face, and Corrina tucked a thick rug around her legs and middle.

"It is a horseless phaeton, miss, and very swift and nimble, for it is fuelled by a great electric battery. Should you need it, I've a parasol to shade you from the sun and wind."

"Oh, I won't have need, Corrina, I love such sensations!" The phaeton started forwards, and Elvie heard the wheels turn on the cobblestones. "A horseless—heavens! Not one sound from a horse. And that hum!"

"It is a fine mechanical sound, is it not? We leave your home, miss," Ahmet stated in a grand tone above her. "And now will ride towards the South Bank, then on for Kensington and Old Brompton."

Elvie clapped her hands in delight.

There were few places she'd visited outside of the Institute, and to know where she was during a journey, she needed the passing surroundings described. But Ellie, due to the very literal information given her by her unique perceptions and her own lack of poetic expression, could only distinguish places as simply "decrepit," "respectable," or "quite hoity-toit." Ahmet delved deeper, inspiring solemnity when he described impoverished settings and people, and then curiosity and delight with his livelier portrayals of healthier surroundings. If he were given to hyperbole, Elvie did not care for the time being, for as a blind person dependent on precise knowledge, truths stripped to their simplest forms were always essential. However, she appreciated his earnestness to entertain.

In passing St Paul's, which Elvie understood was across the Thames in a "very far distance," he remarked on the dome's great height, the stone lantern atop it, then the ball that topped the lantern, and finally the cross that sat upon the ball.

"And from that lantern, I may 'look' upon all of London, Ahmet? I have never understood this city's size," Elvie said.

"Form the measure in your mind in this way, miss: if your skirt, laid flat, were all of London, and you were an ant walking upon it, you might encounter tiny buttons, for the skirt is covered in them. To an ant, wouldn't a button be like a building? Thus, miss, as an ant walking, you might pass button after button, and thereby fathom the entirety of the London that we speak of."

Elvie laughed in both surprise and wonder. How perfect were his descriptions!

They crossed Westminster Bridge, and Ahmet paused in speaking so that she might enjoy the roar of the wind and the rhythmic splashing of waves that broke against the shore beneath the embankment. They slowed by Great Westminster Clock from which Big Ben sounded the hour, much to Elvie's glee; gained speed past the Houses of Parliament; sped by St James's Park, Buckingham Palace and its gardens; skirted Hyde Park, and then entered the area known as South Kensington, in which the hamlet of Brompton nestled. Ahmet announced their entry into the hamlet, and Elvie noted that they'd long left the sounds of London's active, noisy centre behind.

"Here we've great houses, inns, schools for girls, Holy Trinity Church, and Brompton's Little Oratory," Ahmet said. "We pass the Hoop and Toy now, miss, an affable tavern with a pleasant snug frequented by good ladies."

"Oh, this air," Elvie exclaimed.

"We are in the midst of trees, and there are nurseries and market gardens in Old Brompton still, miss," Corrina said. Elvie thought by her tone that she smiled.

Cool shadows and warm light played on her face from the tree canopy they drove beneath. Ahmet described the old carriage avenue they followed, the personalities of the cottages and large houses they passed, noted which were secluded, and pointed out the residences of a poetess, painter, playwright, and songstress.

"Many artists reside in Old Brompton, miss, and one may find a few who wield the chisel besides our good lady," Ahmet said.

"How I look forward to experiencing your lady's work," Elvie said.

"You will find our house and grounds most pleasing, miss, and suitable for a young woman like yourself. You'll be very happy."

"Ahmet," Corrina said, and Elvie was surprised to catch the warning note in her quiet tone. "We are here," she then said as the phaeton slowed, and Elvie's heart leapt to her throat in anxiety and excitement.

Ahmet bade farewell as Elvie disembarked and told her that Alexys raised her hat in her direction. Corrina took Elvie's arm and led her to the house, softly describing the steps, entrance, and vestibule they approached. Elvie heard far-off voices from within and thought they belonged to the other guests. She hoped she'd arrived with ample time to enjoy the marble garden.

"Ahmet said that I would be comfortable here," Elvie began in a questioning tone.

"Ahmet is very proud of our lady's home, miss," Corrina said. "It has an aviary, conservatory, library, the marble garden, and, of course, our lady's sculpting studio. We also enjoy many modern conveniences, like the plumbing and boilers for our bathing room." She said the last with a fond note that Elvie found intriguing. "Here are the front steps, miss, and here also is Adara, who greets you at the entrance, our vestibulum." Corrina helped Elvie step up. "She is keeper of our lady's house."

"And the lady of the house?" Elvie queried.

"*Khaíre*, Miss Chaisty," said a woman who Elvie assumed was Adara, and her voice, unlike Corrina's, was formal and purposeful, with strength like an orator's. "Our lady has unfortunately been detained away, or else she would have been here to bid you welcome. But please, let us refresh you after your ride and introduce you to the pleasures of the garden. While in enjoyment of our sculptures, our lady will then join you."

Elvie, though disappointed at the news of her hostess's delay, could not help a little shiver of anticipation. Her excitement renewed, she allowed the women to lead her farther into the house.

Helia's foot hit the flat cement rooftop outside the window. It was a mere roof, not a balcony, and a low parapet separated a misstep from the street below. Four straining men held the monocled woman by the parapet's edge while Stavros approached, holding aloft a metal syringe. Helia looked from him to the chest of the woman and saw she still bore her own. Ellie brought her arm and blackthorn down on Stavros's knuckles.

"Argh!" he cried, the syringe dropping, and Ellie swung her stick wide, clipping the chin of one of the straining men. His head snapped back, and she whipped her stick down, clubbing another man's knee.

"Ah!" he uttered, clutching his injury.

Stavros scrambled for the fallen syringe and Helia leapt, landing on him. He struggled as she tangled with his limbs and coat, then threw her off and with syringe in hand, scurried for the edge. He jumped over the parapet, his feet striking a surface only a storey down—Helia thought it the balcony below. The monocled woman shrugged off the remaining men. Ellie clubbed another just as the woman reached for her mask.

Helia jumped upon Ellie and engulfed her head with her arms. Smothering her against her breast and hoping she'd blocked all of her friend's unique senses, Helia screwed her eyes shut.

Nothing sounded on the rooftop but her own frantic breathing. She strained to listen. Then a soft, deliberate step landed. Helia peeked.

Lady Thanatou stood upon the parapet, her mask and monocle donned. She looked down at Helia, her blue eye glaring. She leapt. Helia let go of Ellie and rushed to lean over the parapet edge. Lady Thanatou landed upon the walk, five storeys down, her body compressing. With one sleek move she hopped from the walk into the electric buggy. She settled, leaned on the tiller, and drove the vehicle away.

"My *hat*, Helia! Lord above, did you ruin me hat?" Ellie cried behind her. When Helia looked back, Ellie had doffed her hat and was examining the proud pheasant feathers and brim with her fingers. Helia lifted herself from the parapet and looked around. Four men had been turned to stone.

Three were in states of falling, rising, or lying prone, either from Ellie's blows or from being thrown down. She turned to the man nearest her. His fist was raised in anger, his gaze still enraged. She thought of men on the battlefield, facing an aegis with a visage meant to give terror.

"Best y'not do that," Ellie said, and Helia halted from touching the man's marble face. "They're still livin', though their light fades fast. I'll wager she won't return in 'er buggy to bring 'em back to breathin', and I don't fault 'er for that decision."

Helia dropped her hand. "She led them all out here, Ellie, and didn't try to turn them into stone inside."

"Of course, Helia. She had to make them think they cornered 'er, didn't she? No way out. But havin' read 'er impressive fall, I'd say that she could 'ave flung these fellows 'cross the street to the next rooftop. Our interruption might have ruined 'er chance to grab whatever Stavros meant to jab 'er with. She certainly dropped 'er pretence once he ran way. But now, well. Now I know 'er measure."

Helia turned away from the stone man. Ellie wore her hat once more and was reading her pocket watch with her fingers. She put it away.

"She's meant to be at 'er garden party, Helia. The one Elvie was invited to. Let's pursue." Ellie turned for the window, dismissing the dead men as if they were mere gargoyle statues.

Helia climbed in after her. "We'll go to her home, but not to confront her, Ellie. I want to learn more. Knowledge can place us on better footing."

"You want to investigate further. Speak to 'er servants and such." Ellie's back was stiff as she walked out the room. Helia could imagine her mental snort.

"Ellie, while you were chasing her here, did you try speaking to her? Of course you did. And did she answer? Of course she didn't. We're mere insects to one like herself. It would help if we knew how to communicate with such a goddess." She came abreast as they walked down the gallery.

"Goddess! I was thinking she were more a mute, Helia. A dangerous one at that."

"In concern for your friend, we haven't much to challenge the lady with, Ellie. Dolly Teegan chose her fate. Those men attacked, and surely would have again if revived. And the custodian? He is still alive. These actions seem not so very evil."

"True. I'm arrivin' closer to such a conclusion. But that doesn't mean I can't enquire as to 'er intentions, Helia. I witnessed the interest she had for Elvie." Ellie stopped before a gate, and as if guessing at the Up and Down buttons on the wall panel, settled on pushing the bottom one. "You know that in my work I take care not to make light of such attentions."

"I understand, Ellie. But for now, your friend is safe at the Institute. Which gives us time to prepare. After this experience, I should emulate the very sensible psychic detective, Mrs Elle Black, and acquire a hand mirror."

The peacock screamed below, and Helia's hands flew up once more. Irritated by the creature, she moved for the railing and looked down. Teegan still stood before Dolly's marble, hands clasped and body motionless. Helia bowed her head.

The ascension room arrived, and Ellie opened the gate.

"When I was in the basement, the kitchen maid explained that this contraption is used solely for transportin' the marbles," she said as Helia joined her in the room. "The museum's is applied for the same. Guess we spoiled that purpose, heh-heh!" She touched beside the labeled buttons, as if counting them, then chose the one for the ground floor. "Helia, yer mad laugh is missin' from this conversation."

"I know, Ellie. I'm just wondering if that Stavros is still here."

"A fiery fellow. He ran," Ellie said.

"Yes. Strange tactic for a goddess hunter."

"Is that what we are, Helia?"

"I hope not," Helia said.

The room swiftly descended.

CHAPTER FIVE

"Miss Chaisty, please let us care for your walking stick," Adara said, her respectful tone nearly sounding like a polite order. "For touching within the garden would be best with both hands."

"Oh yes! Please. My stick is Canadian diamond willow," Elvie said, running her hand along the diamond grooves. "Hasn't it a lovely pattern?"

"It is beautiful," Adara said, taking the stick. "Corrina will be your guide and companion within. Call on both of us for anything you require. Now come."

Arm in arm with Corrina, Elvie traveled with the women down the vestibule, and Elvie thought it tall, for their steps echoed, and at intervals she felt the warmth that meant sunlight entered. But it seemed to come from very high or, when she raised her face to better feel it, from openings in the ceiling. Wind chimes tinkled in the distance, and the murmur of people conversing grew. When she and Corrina came to a stop, Elvie noted a light breeze on her face, smelled plants, heard a fountain's gentle flow, and determined they had reached an outdoor space. People spoke and stepped to and fro around her, and she wondered in brief apprehension what manner of company she was in, for the voices were distinctly cultured. She knew, from the titter of female shoppers when she and Sarah visited a department store, that she was not considered very well dressed.

She poked beneath her spectacles at her right glass eye, hoping it faced the correct direction, then dismissed such self-consciousness, for she had been invited by the hostess, after all, and intended to enjoy herself as much as possible.

"Corrina, where are we standing presently?" she asked and adjusted her spectacles.

"We stand, miss," Corrina said with quiet earnestness, "within the portico of the peristylium, our peristyle garden. I neglected to explain that this home was built one hundred years ago by an admirer of Roman villas, though the main body of the house has storeys containing the English-style rooms. Therefore, miss, a portico is a roofed arcade, supported by columns, and the portico surrounds a rectangular space. In that airy space lies the peristyle garden."

"This is wonderful," Elvie said and squeezed Corrina's arm in enthusiasm.

"To keep our lady's latest sculptures a mystery, the area we wait in is obscured by a partition. Soon, we will all emerge to enjoy her exhibit. Would you like refreshment, miss? We serve teas of spring water infused with violets and honeysuckle, and another of the hibiscus flower."

"Hibiscus," Elvie said. "I wish to try that, Corrina."

While Elvie enjoyed the fruity, floral flavour of sweet hibiscus tea, someone tapped a drinking glass and all the voices stilled.

"Welcome," Adara greeted, her projected voice commanding attention, and Elvie enjoyed her clear pronunciations, wondering if she had ever performed on the stage. "Lady Thanatou rejoices that you join her in celebration of her latest creations, and that you are here to appreciate them, to know them, by your sense of touch alone. Let *haphê* now begin."

Guests shuffled about, and several gave low, hushed exclamations while others fussed and some laughed in amusement.

"What is happening?" Elvie asked.

"The guests are being blindfolded, miss," Corrina said. "And each will be led into the marble garden by an attendant for *haphê*, the touching."

"Oh, how I've anticipated this!" Elvie exclaimed, and Corrina led her forwards. Elvie noted their emergence from the arcade by the return of the sun's warmth and heard guests before and behind her, moving with hesitance. Someone giggled, clearly nervous. Wind chimes again tinkled, and Elvie listened to mark their distance, for she heard several different ones, in four directions, and wondered if they marked the four sides of the peristyle garden. When Corrina brought her to a stop, she realised she was separated from the other guests, and by the sounds of their unsure steps and voices, thought them all scattered. More nervous laughter and exclamations ensued as each person dealt with his or her temporary blindness. A man amiably chatted to his attendant, his commentary nonstop. Elvie listened, and imagined the distances between all of them.

"Miss?" Corrina said beside her.

"I am ready," Elvie said, smiling. "Let us begin."

The first figure she touched was small, no taller than the

length of her hand. It was the naive carving of a woman, with featureless face and simple round head. Its breasts, thighs, and buttocks were rotund and the hips wide, with little arms resting on its heavy breasts.

"Oh, how—a mother figure!" Elvie exclaimed, feeling the big belly. "No, not quite. This is more a well-fed lady. Such buttocks. Does she have a name, Corrina?"

"It is a *Venus*, miss, a style of figurine said to be a remnant of a prehistoric fertility cult."

"Prehistoric? Goodness, I may drop it," Elvie said, trying to hand the figurine back.

"Oh no, miss, please enjoy it. Our lady fashioned this copy of the original, and she is most precise."

"Is she? I love precision," Elvie said. She tapped the prominent buttocks and giggled.

But while exploring the Venus more, feeling the clear incision of a vulva beneath the round belly, she heard the other guests around the garden and noted their hushed sounds. Women were prone to exclamations of "oh my!", "how beautiful," or "remarkable," but men barely said a word, except for one fellow, who simply muttered, "lovely, lovely". When Elvie stood still, holding the Venus like a doll, she began to discern the whispers of couples; it made sense, she realised, that lovers might want to enjoy this unique garden event together. Two near her giggled, and she thought their whispers coy.

"Would you like to explore another, miss?"

"Oh yes," Elvie said, holding the Venus out.

The next sculpture Corrina led her to, Elvie recognised as an ideal male nude from the straining muscles beneath her hands—the lack of head and arms indicating it might be a mere torso, though of a tall, sizeable man. She ran her fingers down the arching figure's sides to grip its prominent oblique muscles and giggled, realising she should not blame her fellow guests for naughty behaviour. Hugging the flexed back to her, she attempted to gauge the power exerted by the figure's pose, and thought it in the midst of a mighty struggle. She reached around and traced her fingers down the pronounced Adonis line leading to the groin; the torso still retained the tops of its muscular thighs and its sexual organ. But the thighs had cracks and had been fitted back together; when she knelt to feel more, she found his legs grown out of a rough base, all of crevices and great cracks. It had been purposely shattered and made whole again.

Elvie rose and brought her hands up to caress the torso's tense shoulders, held high though no arms were present to indicate what the male struggled against.

"This one . . . is mature of body, and unlike the usual, beautiful youth. He might have been—how do the Americans say it? Rugged. He is power, being tested. And perhaps I speculate too much in thinking this the body of an accomplished man."

"Accomplished, miss?"

"A father of many children; a fellow of deeds. A man of change." Elvie traced the spine down to the flexed buttocks, thrust out to support the torso's mysterious action.

"The model for this torso was indeed a 'rugged' man, miss. Our lady asked that he shave all his body hair. And his beard."

At that, Elvie covered her mouth and laughed, and she hoped her mirth didn't distract the other guests. She decided not to enquire as to the fate of the man's head of hair. "And his profession?"

"Miss, that is meant to be a secret, but our lady allows

that you may know this much: he is presently a Secret Commission agent."

Elvie felt along the torso's back again, and the great pressure on the shoulders. *A man not struggling, but lifting. Or upholding. And oh so hirsute.* "And yet his thighs are shattered," she mused. "He stands on unsteady ground." Elvie put her hands together, delighted. "Well," she said, moving to the torso's front. She smiled and rested her hands on its chest. "I am very pleased to meet you, Mr Atlas."

Atlas thus identified, Corrina led Elvie to the nude torso of a woman: curvaceous, broad of shoulders, and with her garments pulled down, revealing her dimpled buttocks.

"How callipygian," Elvie cooed, kneeling to run her hands along the shapely, sleek slopes.

"Why, so it is, miss," Corrina said with quiet humour. "For this one is called the *Kallipygos.*"

Elvie briefly laid her cheek against the sculpture's perfect cheeks, then rose to move around to the front, where the pulled-down garments revealed the marble's smooth mons veneris. Elvie hugged the figure, thinking it very womanly yet quite the sturdy, strong female, with a breadth to her chest and a smallness to her waist that thrilled her. She studied the breasts. They were not of the classical artistic ideal: pert, peaked, and untouched by gravity. Instead, they were full and heavy—fruitlike, Elvie thought—and sat pleasingly upon the chest. There was even a light incision on each to indicate the large areola mammaes surrounding the nipples.

"Oh, I didn't know they could be this big," Elvie said under her breath as she traced the circles. She caught whispers from a couple close by.

"Feel it, his fingers pressed into her flesh," a man urgently said. A woman murmured, and her incoherent sound seemed delighted.

Elvie stood still, hands on the torso's breasts, and listened to the garden. Most all the other guests had fallen silent, even the muttering man. A breeze sent the wind chimes tinkling, and plants rustled.

"Corrina," Elvie asked, her voice low. "Is most of your lady's work . . . provocative?"

"Miss, do you find what I've shown you to be so?" Corrina's tone was also soft.

"Corrina, no, this and the Atlas are beautiful; so aesthetically pleasing. I just wonder why the other guests, whether artists or perhaps buyers? Have fallen into deeper absorption." She smiled and let her hands wander down the torso's front, loving the indentations of a strong abdomen. "It is a compliment to our hostess's work that it captivates her audience so."

"You are correct, miss. There are buyers here for certain works. Our lady has fashioned pieces like *Leda and Her Swan*, the *Satyr and the Maenad*; *Apollo and Hyacinth*."

"Such as I would never encounter in Room 84 of the British Museum," Elvie said, kneeling to touch lower. "They do sound like popular themes."

"They are, miss, and provocative, as you've discerned. But some are not merely so. I see secrets in the *Veiled Dancer*, hunger in *The Siren*, curled around her drowning man. And there is—" Corrina paused. "And perhaps I've said too much. My lady did not wish to . . . overwhelm you, miss, but have you enjoy pleasing works."

"They are, very pleasing." Elvie rose, having discovered that the sculpture ended at the knees, its garments pooling. "You are so lovely," she sighed to it. Had it a head, she would have kissed it. She touched its chest one last time. "Corrina, I've now learned more than I've ever been allowed, and for that I'm grateful. But now I'm curious."

"Miss?"

Elvie tickled the female torso's navel. "What figure here does your mistress greatly favour?"

———

Corrina brought Elvie to a sculpture that was neither provocative nor one to elicit intimate whispers. It was a lifesize male figure, nude, with a body less the muscular ideal but very much that of a solid, strong man's—Elvie thought, perhaps of the common man. He sat upon his base supported by one hand, his manner weary, his hair thick, and his bowed head heavy. He had a moustache, and a ring adornment circling his neck that Corrina called a "torc." Thus identified, Elvie knew the man was Celtic. She felt all his surfaces until she found the cause of his body's surrender: a wound bled drops beneath his ribs. Lying under him was his abandoned sword, belt, and a curved trumpet.

"He is dying," Elvie said.

"He is, miss. Our lady finds satisfaction in copying antiquities, and this is one such piece. He is the *Dying Galatian*, though he is more well known as the *Dying Gladiator*."

Elvie cupped the man's bowed head. "And is it very precise? Is that why your mistress favours it?"

"I cannot say why my lady is fond of the *Dying Galatian*, miss. But I know her to copy a work even to its faults and errors."

Elvie remembered the sure hands of the women rapidly copying the paintings in the National Gallery, their intensity of focus and uncanny ability to somehow *know* the works before them, charging the very air. She shivered.

"Oh, miss, are you cold?" Corrina said in concern.

"N-no, Corrina." Elvie laughed. "I am not that at all." She touched the *Dying Galatian* a last time and silently bade it farewell. "What shall I know next?"

The figure Corrina led her to next was female and seemed the typical beautiful maiden; Elvie knew it by feeling the breasts first. But when she ran her hands down the slender arms, she discovered manacles on the wrists. The figure's hands were held in modesty before her mons veneris, as if to shield herself, and chain links dangled from her shackles. Elvie brought her hands up to feel the face. It looked away and down, its fine nose, brow, and lips those of a fresh-faced girl, her long hair gathered and pinned up. Though the face bore the eternal calm that sculptures typically had, Elvie thought the line of the brows sad.

"Corrina, is this a copy of the *Greek Slave?*" Elvie whispered.

"No, miss, it is not of Hiram Powers's famous piece. This one is an individual, and simply called *The Slave.*"

"I thought so . . . this face, it is modern. And young." Elvie held the face, wondering. She then ran her hands down to the feet, finding the girl entirely nude, and moved behind her to investigate further. Her touch began at the ankles, and as she raised her hands, her fingers encountered marks on the sculpture's calves.

Elvie swallowed. She traced the long, thin marks and recalled Mrs Darby's penny-dread stories of whippings. She moved up and found more on the back of the thighs. She paused beneath the buttocks.

"I can't go on," Elvie said.

"I understand, miss." Corrina touched Elvie to help her up.

"But I should," Elvie said. "This." She touched the marks on the thighs. "For her to model for this. The statement has been made and should be recognised, as with Hiram Powers's *Greek Slave*." She moved her hands up. With each touch, she slowly rose.

Elvie found every hurt and caressed it, along the curve of the girl's behind and across her back, lines drawn by a contemptuous, cruel hand. If the statue had been alive, Elvie would have said, "How very brave you are." She ended her touch at the nape, then reached over and caressed the sculpture's cheek. She fetched her handkerchief from her sleeve and dabbed the corners of her eye sockets.

"You are so thorough in your appreciation, miss." Corrina's voice held quiet admiration.

Elvie sniffed her sadness away, then smiled. "Yet, Corrina, I may have taken too much time. I can hear guests moving from object to object. Should I hurry?"

"No, miss, please grace us with your fullest appreciation. One afternoon is not enough to experience all within my lady's garden. But there is time for you to enjoy two more works, if you are not weary."

"I am full of vigour, Corrina, and may I make a request?" She reached for Corrina and felt her take her hand. "Please take me to the two pieces you greatly favour."

—

Elvie was uncertain if she was the last to leave the garden proper, but other guests had finished and were enjoying refreshments. She could hear their activity even as Corrina walked her towards them. They stepped once more into the portico area, the absence of sun and the echo of their steps marking their entrance into the arcade. More paces, and they entered a room Corrina called the *exedra*, or garden room. By the sounds of voices bouncing off the walls, Elvie felt it to be a great room, one in which the fragrance of poured wine wafted. Some people laughed, while others engaged in conversations, discussing the pieces or more boorishly—she thought—their own private matters. Someone bumped into her, and Elvie started.

"Pardon me, why—hello! You're a sight! That is, if you could see yourself," a young man said, cheeky, and his breath smelled of wine. Elvie adjusted her spectacles and doubted he was truly drunk. When he'd jostled her, her first thought had been for her diamond willow so that she might accidentally knock him.

"I beg your pardon," she said. "I believe you've lost your blindfold. And what may you be referring to?"

"Well—your funny eyes! Misplaced the real ones, have you?"

Oh, witty, Elvie thought sourly. "I assure you, sir, I haven't. They currently reside in a jar."

"A jar! But why?"

"Why, for medical study, of course! The pathogenesis of my particular eye disease was described to me as a malignant ocular neoplasm. In other words, a *tumour oculorum*. If my eyes had not been enucleated, the tumours would have grown to infect my brain."

"I see," the man said. "How extraordinary! Will you excuse me?" She heard him move away and then exclaim at the sight of someone else.

He did ask, the lout, Elvie thought, peeved.

"I apologise for that man's behaviour, miss," Corinna said, her voice low. "He is the son of one of our guests, and of little merit."

"It's not your fault he's also missing his brain, Corinna," Elvie said, "and then misplaced his brain jar." A woman suddenly stepped too near, her heels landing sharply, and as her skirts swished by, Elvie stilled in case others followed her.

"But she can't just vanish for good. I need her vocal testimonial. My exposé for the *Reformer* will suffer, and naught will come of it," the woman said.

"We assure you, Miss Le Bon, you will have more than that," Adara said, her tone placating.

The two moved on, and Elvie lost their further words in the murmuring of the gathering.

The Reformer? Elvie thought in surprise. Then the woman who spoke was the advocate, Miss Annie Le Bon. Elvie was rather pleased to learn of the activist's presence, and if opportunity allowed, she wouldn't mind introducing herself to compliment Miss Le Bon on her controversial publication, *Birth Control for All.* But any wonderment she had of why a social reformer like Miss Le Bon was present at an artistic event fled when Corinna took her hands.

"Miss, please come this way. You've one more marble to meet, and it is our lady's most beloved," she said warmly.

She led Elvie to a place where they had to step up, and when she asked where they were standing, Corrina explained it was a dais surrounded by tall ferns. Elvie could still hear guests talking, and concluded that though she and Corrina were possibly secluded, they remained in the midst of the party.

"Our lady has this treasure obscured from casual gazes. One needs to part the fern fronds to see, for the piece is meant to retain its mystery. But you are welcomed to know it, miss, by touch."

"What an honour," Elvie said in a hushed voice. "But what is this treasure, Corrina?" Corrina led Elvie's hands to the cool marble shoulders of a figure her own height.

"It is a woman, miss."

Elvie exhaled, delighted. But after the experience of the one called *The Slave*, she had to know. She felt her way around and then ran her hands down the sculpture's back to take in the entirety of her stance, her bearing. The body rested contrapposto, the shoulders back and her arms at her sides. Elvie moved to the front, feeling the features of the face, then trailed her palms and fingers down. Though the sculpture's head was bowed, it was as though she regarded one who knelt before her. By her pure nudity, she was a woman made noble. Her hands opened at her sides, palms out, presenting herself as both receiver and bestower. Calm and grave seemed her gaze, the brow's attitude peaceful, the softened mouth—barely hinting at a smile. Her long hair curtained the sides of her face, giving her an aspect of dignity and modesty, though, Elvie thought, more like one who owned mystery. Elvie ran her hands up to feel the sculpture's features again, the shapes of nose, lips, eyes, and cheeks.

This is not a face fashioned after the ideal. This is an individual.

And yet it was a face from which the classical ideal might have been based. Elvie traced the arched brows, full mouth, and round chin of a beautiful woman.

"You," Elvie said.

"Miss?" Corrina asked.

Elvie held the sculpture's face, then touched her forehead to its forehead and placed her sleeve at the sculpture's shoulder. She slowly brushed her sleeve down, creating a soft sound.

Shhhhhussshh

Elvie shuddered, tingles emanating from her scalp and down her neck. Her cuff left the tip of the sculpture's breast, and she smiled.

"She's here," a woman said, admiration in her voice. Elvie raised her head.

"I'm surprised that she deigned to walk among us," another woman murmured drily.

"I'll try to make introductions," a man whispered to someone. "But—she is not one who's easily approached."

Then Elvie smelled it: roses, decadent and rich, borne upon frankincense and myrrh. She breathed and heard the soft, deliberate approach of a woman's step. They were knowing steps. Measured. They were like—

Like what? Elvie thought. *Like the cat's paws stepping for the bird.*

Elvie poked behind her spectacles at her right glass eye and turned. She gripped the statue's hip as fronds rustled and the steps ceased near her.

"She was a *hetaera*," a woman said in a soft voice. "Her name was Thana."

Elvie inhaled. The woman spoke in a low tone, touched by a Mediterranean accent. Hers was a full-bodied voice. Cool, majestic. Quiet-spoken.

You match the perfume, Elvie thought. "This marble is of Thana?"

"Yes."

"She is beautiful. I am Miss Elvie Chaisty. How do you do?"

"*Aspázdomai*, Elvie," the woman said, her tone deep, and Elvie did not know if the word was a greeting or a comment.

Elvie did not hold out her hand, though she always attempted, even if it meant accidentally putting her hand where she shouldn't. Instead, it remained on the statue's hip and the other in the crevice on the other side, between Thana's arm and indentation of waist. In that way, she hid the tremor in her hands.

"*Aspázdomai*," she said in return.

She detected a very slight sound. It was the sound lips made when they stretched over teeth.

"I am *Despoina* Thanatou," the woman gave. "In your language that is *lady*, or mistress of this house."

"You are my . . . the sculptress. Thank you for your invitation. As we've never been properly introduced, I found this so unexpected."

"I understand. I wanted to ask your forgiveness for disturbing you at the museum."

Elvie's cheeks heated. "You witnessed my—and knew to—" she said. "Somehow you knew." She nervously held Thana. "And I was pleased by it."

She noted that faint sound again. Elvie wanted to reach out and feel if the sculptress smiled.

"I created this garden for one like you, Elvie," the lady said. "It pleases me to have you here."

Elvie grinned, delighted. "I love your work. It's so beautiful, so knowing! Is Thana one of your older works?"

"I made her, yes."

"Yet your name is also 'Thana.' In that it is 'Thanatou,'" Elvie said in curiosity.

"I named myself after my beloved, yes."

Elvie liked how the sculptress pronounced *yes*. It had a quiet gravity, the weight of affirmation. It was unlike the casual promise given the word when spoken by herself and her fellow Britons.

"I first saw you, little *kore*, a week ago, at the museum," the sculptress added.

"What? I am not a *kore*," Elvie protested. She let go of Thana's waist. She was rather taken aback by the casually spoken endearment—if that was what it was. She was uncertain whether she liked being called a stone maiden; perhaps Greek women tended to such familiarity. "Well, I confess to having been aware of you too, Lady Thanatou, during that visit. You are singular in your choice of perfume."

The sculptress hummed. Elvie thought it a pleased sound.

"Why do you wear eyes today?" the lady suddenly asked.

"I—to look acceptable, I suppose," Elvie said. "They're a lovely pair, and I'm told their colour is sky-blue."

She heard a soft intake of breath and recognised the sound. It was the sort she heard from proper women attempting to suppress mirth.

Elvie thought of Sarah and had a sour realisation. "My ocular prostheses don't match, do they?" she said.

The sculptress did not answer. Elvie could detect no breathing and determined that the lady was holding her breath.

"Oh, it's utter nonsense," Elvie said.

She removed and folded her spectacles, found the latch pin on her breast to hook them on, then reached into her right eye socket and pried the glass out. It popped out between her fingers and she held it firmly.

"Heavens!" a woman cried nearby, fronds rustling.

She heard a heavy scrape on the floor as though the peeper had tottered. More feet moved and several male voices exclaimed. But what gratified her was the sound before her: breathy, husky, and delighted. Elvie didn't mind the sculptress's mirth. Her own mouth widened in return. She pocketed the right eye and then reached up to poke out the left one. Soon, she held that too between her fingers, and her relaxed eyelid shrank and nearly shut. Her lids, no longer stretched wide for the glass, resumed their accustomed positions, revealing slits.

"There," she said in relief. "Nothing but flesh to see."

"May I look at your eye?" the sculptress said.

Elvie hesitated, unsure if the lady referred to her eye socket or the glass. She held the prosthesis up between her fingertips, and Lady Thanatou gently plucked it.

"It is German glass," Elvie said.

"Superior to an eye made of gold, hung with gold thread," the sculptress softly said.

Elvie wondered what gold was like. In the museum, gold objects were stored behind glass. She hadn't a chance to touch the substance, but she understood it to be precious. A curator described "gold" as the brightest sunbeam possible made solid. Whatever *bright* meant. She felt the eye pressed back into her palm and automatically clasped the fingers around it. The sculptress's bare fingers were roughened like a labourer's and warm and firm. Very steady and firm. The touch gave her a thrill, and Elvie wanted to play with those fingers as she had done as a child with her father's.

How strong they are, she thought, awed.

And just like a child with her parent's fingers, she surmised that she might not have the power to budge the sculptress's. But they relaxed in her grasp, long and slender, and their touch, tender. Her heart beat faster.

The sculptress removed her hand. "I will return," she whispered to Elvie, and then she was gone.

Elvie held her glass eye and felt the air with her free hand. In the space of a scant breath, Lady Thanatou had managed to disappear. Corrina murmured "Miss" next to her and took her arm.

Did I do something wrong? Elvie thought in dismay.

A woman's strident voice sounded from the garden. Elvie heard people speak in low voices, questioning the noise, and then feet and bodies moved as if to gather where the altercation could be observed.

"What is happening?" Elvie said, and Corrina helped her emerge from the dais.

"And I said, remove it at once," the same loud voice ordered.

"A late guest has entered the garden without a blindfold, miss. A countess."

"Who commissioned this? If you don't remove it, I'll have it destroyed," the countess threatened.

"What?" Elvie gasped.

"She has recognised the marble called *The Slave*," Corrina said quietly. "For the girl resembling that marble was her unwilling plaything."

"Her—oh," Elvie whispered. "You mean . . . oh." She felt ill at the thought.

"You confess to knowing this likeness, then? She wanted to be free of you," Adara said, her weighted tone like a court's formal accusation.

"What? You speak nonsense!"

"We witnessed her pain," Adara said. "She told us what you did to her."

The countess laughed. "The little liar."

"What you did many times." Adara's tone grew cold. "There is a difference between cruelty and lust. Your society shall know that of you, soon."

"Do not threaten me," the countess menaced. Elvie strained to hear more, but the countess chose not to speak further. A chill grew, and Elvie shivered.

"Now she comes," a man breathlessly exclaimed.

"Such a look Lady Thanatou gives her," a woman whispered, her voice smug.

She listened as a woman spun on her heel, scraping stone and swishing her skirts. A cane struck the arcade floor, loud and sharp, violently biting the stone. The angry sound grew distant. Then the guests' murmuring rose, signalling the countess's possible departure.

"That Lady Thanatou," a man said eagerly, "didn't have to say a word!"

"What a treat, to witness that," a young woman said with glee.

"Oh, what just happened?" Elvie fretted. "That countess sounds vindictive!"

"Do not worry, miss," Corrina assured, her voice low. "Our lady will ruin her."

"Is that what Adara referred to?"

"Yes, miss. The girl who was made that woman's toy had a last request. We will continue to display her marble. The countess will be shamed before her own society, and not for pity of the girl, but because the countess could not hide her perversions."

"What a feat." Elvie drew breath at the thought. "It's so . . . I hope that causes the ruin the girl intends. But is the girl herself safe, Corrina? From that terrible woman?"

"Yes, miss. She is safe now, forever."

CHAPTER SIX

Five minutes distance from the house of Lady Thanatou, Ellie and Helia sat behind the frosted glass of the Hoop and Toy's snug, enjoying an afternoon meal. Not that Ellie had wanted to make the stop, but where Helia was concerned, all delays during an investigation had a purpose.

Before them sat Miss Annie Le Bon, whom Helia had recognised while the woman rode her wheel quickly away from the very address Ellie had all intentions of reaching. Instead, Helia made the driver turn around so she could hail Miss Le Bon, cajole her to halt, and then invite her to the Hoop and Toy. Ellie would have begrudged the delay except for one thing: Miss Le Bon wrote about social injustices, not artists's garden fêtes. Even if Helia's suspicion of Miss Le Bon's purpose in Old Brompton turned out to be incorrect, it at least earned Ellie a porkpie with ale, and Miss Le Bon a tumbler of brandy and a chop she'd yet to touch. Instead, she smoked a cigarette along with Helia and seemed to give Helia — as far as Ellie could tell of the woman's protective life-glow — a very cool and wary regard.

Miss Le Bon was square of shoulder, with sturdy limbs and hands and a stern aspect, though Ellie thought her attitude less of the street and more tempered by upper-class rearing. And like certain learned, modern women, she was an activist and social reformer, with a special interest in exposing sexual slavery. But unlike the women and men of the rescue missions, her personal crusades were more motivated by secular values. Ellie enjoyed making the flustered Mrs Darby read aloud the educational penny pamphlets Miss Le Bon published, for she thought it very necessary that Elvie and their fellow boarders understand matters like female contraceptives.

"Annie," Helia said, then exhaled smoke. "You say you've never met Lady Thanatou, but you attended this marble garden event because you were mysteriously informed that it would help your present investigation?"

"That was what I was told. I'm in the midst of exposing a charity-girl school here in Brompton, one I suspect of selling girls to despicable gentry like yourself, Helia."

Ellie coughed on a bite of her porkpie.

"I . . . admit to contributing to certain injustices in the past," Helia said as she tapped her cigarette into her ash box. "But Annie, I seek to make amends now."

"All you write about are the antics of those supernatural agents, Helia, and do nothing for our girl captives."

"Annie, did you learn what you needed at the garden event?"

"I did," Annie said with satisfaction. "Evidence that confirms Countess Ogfrey for the wicked woman she is. She owns the school, you see, and likes to procure the girls for herself. One of her captives was Rose Batts, whose disappearance from the school I was investigating. Somehow, Rose found sanctuary with Lady Thanatou and has vanished again. But today, a most provocative marble Lady Thanatou has presented, called *The Slave*, was recognised by Countess Ogfrey as being in the image of Rose Batts. There were many at the party who witnessed her admittance."

"An interesting public humiliation," Helia said thoughtfully.

"Yet I doubt it will stop her," Annie said. "Rose Batts left me a written account of what happened to her before disappearing for good. That is all I have, against a countess's word! An exposé based on it is no longer enough. I need—"

"Material suitable for blackmail?" Helia said. "You need to ruin her, Annie. Ogfrey will not stop unless you've something she cannot deny."

"I agree. I need another who can expose her. Surely the countess hasn't kept her cruel hands off a new victim? That is who I need, and she needs to be rescued, now."

"I agree. And Ellie can help you, Annie."

"Wot?" Ellie said, putting down her ale.

Helia chuckled and extinguished her dwindling cigarette. "Sneak into her home and use a bee smoker, Ellie! Just like that time I needed to search a certain duke's home to retrieve damning letters." She nibbled on her fragment of cheddar and sliver of ham.

"Though I've never taken advantage of your bodyguard services, Miss Hench, your reputation preceeds you," Annie said.

"But liberatin' a girl is not like liftin' a packet of letters!" Ellie protested. "I can't perceive through walls, Helia, behind which you know the poor unfortunate will be imprisoned. We'll be ejected long before we can find 'er."

"Not if we use this." Annie pulled out folded papers from her leather satchel. She laid them out. "This map of the house interior, with instructions and the indication of

Ogfrey's secret room, was drawn by Rose Batts herself. And I've this." She presented a hardwood box with mounted lenses. "One especially made to withstand destruction by angry countesses."

"Well now," Ellie said, appraising the camera. "In that, I approve. But I need the map described to me, Miss Le Bon. Helia, I've my fee, as you know, and for such an exercise as this, it shall be tripled."

"Of course, Ellie, I will pay it. But I can't join in this rescue, I'm afraid. I've something else to investigate."

"I thought you wouldn't. Why make an adversary of one of your society when your sister is due to be a countess herself?" Annie said coldly.

"Helene is quite prepared to don male dress so that she might be addressed as 'earl,' Annie, whenever that time should come. But I'm leaving you two because of this." She held up a key dangling a metal tag, engraved with a hotel name and room number. Ellie knew the sighted alphabet well enough to discern the grooved marks: *Osborne's*.

"What will you be doing in Westminster's Adelphi?" Annie said.

"I hope to be questioning a man named Stavros, from whose pocket I picked this, whilst you and Ellie are ruining Countess Olgfrey."

The sculptress's garden event, rather than winding down, became more gay with the flow of wine. Elvie heard the liquid poured and smelled it in the air while someone strummed a stringed instrument. The guests talked animatedly, their tongues loosened not just by wine but by the incident with the countess. Propriety lessened; conversations touched

on vulgar subjects. Before Corrina could introduce her to
others, Elvie asked to be led aside instead. Though some
discussions were humorous, resulting in blasts of laughter,
Elvie felt uncomfortable with the meanspirited chatter.
She'd hoped for more intellectually engaging conversations
for such an artistic gathering, and if there were intellectual
minds about, they harboured their wit and kept silent.
She smelled fruity, heady smoke stronger than cigarettes
and learned water pipes were present. Corrina offered her
cheese and grapes, but Elvie declined, unable to dismiss a
certain, sad conclusion occupying her mind.

"I feel terrible, Corrina," she finally blurted. "Though it
was simply her likeness, I did explore the one called *The
Slave*. I now feel I shouldn't have done it."

"Please do not feel so. You were the sole person allowed to
touch her, miss," Corrina said.

"I . . . really?"

"Yes, for I desired that you know her," the sculptress said,
filling Elvie's senses with her voice and the scent of roses
and frankincense.

"I didn't even hear you approach," Elvie softly exclaimed.
She shuddered as a thrill ran down her back.

The sculptress gave a curt command in Greek and
Corrina left Elvie's side, explaining that she would fetch her
a wrap. Elvie would have protested but she was listening
to—measuring—the sculptress's nearness and the way she
moved.

The sculptress had announced herself in the museum
when she had deliberately stepped closer to Elvie, then
again at Thana's statue. But in reality the sculptress did not
travel like others did, much in the way Ellie did not when
she went into action, immersed in her fluid world. Elvie

suspected then, with an alarm and curiosity that outweighed caution, that somehow her hostess was something more than what might be considered ordinary. But what? Various clues had already been given her: The strength she'd felt in those hands, a pair seemingly imbued with more power than Elvie's touch had ever known. And the manner in which the sculptress moved, more silently than Ellie, who was such a master of her own body. And more quickly. And so perfectly.

Ellie's encountered other kinds amongst us, she recalled, her heart hammering at the thought. She hoped Lady Thanatou wasn't one of the fabled vampyres. She held out her hands, and the lady took hold of them.

No, her fingers are truly warm, Elvie thought in relief, once more experiencing a thrill. She marvelled at the heat in them and wondered if there were such beings as cat people, like those of Bastet, perhaps. She liked cats. "You are quite perfect," she said. "And I shan't be a startled bird, chirrup, and fly away."

"Elvie?" the sculptress said.

"What rose scent are you wearing?" Elvie asked. "It is richer than any I've known."

"It is the Anatolian rose."

"Anatolia."

The sculptress's fingers caressed her own.

"Come experience my studio," she said, her voice low.

"Oh yes."

"Tomorrow. I will send Corrina for you."

"Yes." She had classes to teach, more stockings to knit. But she would rid herself of all obligations to visit the sculptress again. She raised her hand, desiring to touch the lady's face. The sculptress led her searching hand, and her fingers contacted—

"A mask," Elvie said in wonderment, touching the metal. She caressed along it and brushed where hair would be. Instead, she encountered fabric; a snood heavy with contained hair, just as Ellie had described.

Something hissed at her, the sound muffled.

She drew back her hand, surprised. "What?" she softly exclaimed.

The sculptress grasped her hands. "I keep . . . snakes," she said.

"Do you?" Bewildered, Elvie tried to comprehend how the sound had been so near. The lady's hands withdrew. Corrina took Elvie's arm and laid a wrap around her shoulders, then her stick was placed in her hands. Corrina led her away, and Elvie heard the laughing guests left behind while her footsteps and Corrina's echoed in the vestibule.

"It is time to depart, miss," Corrina quietly said.

"Lady Thanatou?" Elvie called.

"*Hypíaine*, Elvie. Until tomorrow," she heard the sculptress bid behind her, and Corrina led Elvie down the vestibule. The entrance doors creaked open, and Elvie listened, even though she knew she would detect nothing more of the sculptress's presence.

CHAPTER SEVEN

Ellie did not indulge in rescue; she'd lived long enough to keep her services simple. The sale of girls, especially of virgins as young as ten or twelve, was longstanding in London, and Ellie did not doubt that Countess Ogfrey would procure another poor soul the next day. Or flee to the continent and resume such habits, out of the reach of troublemakers like Annie Le Bon. But Miss Le Bon's crusade to expose such depravity was for the good of the whole, and Ellie speculated she might see society's improvement on such matters, someday.

Thus she spent her night aiding Miss Le Bon in her daring breach of a countess's home by utilizing Helia's trick of a bee smoker for distraction. Having never worked with Annie Le Bon before, she was pleased to have by her side a level-headed, stalwart companion not easily shaken while Ellie knocked unconscious everyone they encountered, including the house boy. The conclusion to their mission was one unconscious countess, several unconscious servants of the Ogfrey household, and the liberation of one girl, presently also unconscious (though not by Ellie's doing), and wrapped in blankets while she, Ellie, and Annie fled by carriage. They rode across Winchester Bridge with Great Westminster Clock sounding the hour. Ellie marked the sleeping girl across from her and thought on the lattice of disease she'd witnessed flaring from head to toe within the disfigured Countess Ogfrey's body-glow.

"Do you always dose rescued girls with a bit o' soothing syrup, Miss Le Bon?" Ellie asked.

"It makes transport to the doctress easier," Annie said and tucked the blankets tighter around the girl. She sighed. "That went well. Thank you, Miss Hench."

"Well, you did indulge me, Miss Le Bon, by puttin' the servants in them dungeon restraints and devises of the countess's secret room. 'N taking their photographs in that room. 'N keepin' the keys, though I certainly didn't request that of you."

"Perhaps I was too enthusiastic in our efforts to discourage charges brought later against us," Annie said, smiling. She patted the camera on the seat. "Whether the photographs develop successfully or not, what's important is that ogress saw the camera."

"After witnessin' 'er secret chamber, Miss Le Bon, I think what's in yer camera may draw more 'arm to you than protection. Better you not go 'ome but hie yerself to a safe place. Perhaps for a few months. And make them several places. 'Er ogre-ship can still send thugs from 'er grave."

"I understand, Miss Hench, and I agree with your caution. But what makes you think Ogfrey will soon be dead?"

"Well." Ellie scratched her nose. "Yer rescued poppet. A very good doctor will know."

"I . . . see." Annie's tone was grim. "Ogfrey's ruined face

. . . ."

"Aye. She's been sharin' 'er gift of venereal disease. If they haven't yet appeared on the girl, expect chancres."

Annie's life-fire dimmed and she sighed.

"Can't blame Rose Batts for disappearin'," Ellie said.

When the carriage arrived in Southwark, stopping before the Institute of the Blind, Annie had parting words. "Miss Hench, having learned more of Miss Chaisty's situation, I must tell you she ought to beware. The house of Lady Thanatou is another place where women disappear."

"First you tell us Rose Batts found sanctuary with 'er, now you imply the lady's a danger. Which is it, Miss Le Bon?"

"Well, Miss Hench, consider this: is a pagan household indulging in ritualistic practices a safe place? The sculptress, like many of her artist acquaintances, is a hedonist." Annie sniffed. "They frolic and ingest stimulants. But I feel that such a rakish reputation on Lady Thanatou's part veils more serious intentions. One that deceives the naive. A cult's beliefs, Miss Hench, can compromise any woman's safety."

Ellie disembarked and contemplated that as the carriage pulled away. Upon entering the Institute, she found her fellow boarders and Mrs Darby still awake by the drawing room fire, discussing Elvie's own adventure at the marble-garden event.

"Huh," Ellie said as she stood listening to them chatter.

"Hold on, is that smoke I smell?" Sarah said.

"That's me, Sarah," Ellie called.

"Ellie! And where have you been? I thought you'd be chaperoning Elvie to this party," Mrs Darby exclaimed. "Thank our Lord she made it home safely, and no thanks to you."

"I'd another important matter to 'andle, Mrs Darby," Ellie

answered. "'N 'andled well."

"Elvie was doin' a lot of 'andling too today," Alan said and snickered.

"Wish I were rich and lived in a big Brompton home," Sarah sighed. "Elvie could have asked me to chaperone. She's fortunate nothing untoward happened. She was invited by an artist!"

"Yes, yes," Mrs Darby said. "And—and we know how sinful those artists can be!"

"Oh, rot, Mrs Darby," Alan said in a dismissive tone. "Elvie was none the worse, and she returned with choice stories!"

"Elvie was 'appy, then? That's all that matters," Ellie said. "She'd 'ave flown a locked room to go, without my 'elpin'." She departed for the stairs.

"That's because she's a changeling," Sarah said.

Once upstairs, Ellie paused before Elvie's shut door and heard her singing within. Then Elvie began narrating aloud, describing the surfaces of a sculpture, and Ellie knew she was writing in her journal. She turned to go, her heel squeaking upon the floor.

"Who is that? Alan? I'm not writing anything naughty, if that's what you're listening for," Elvie called.

"It's me, Elvie. Good night to you," Ellie said.

"Oh! Good night, Ellie."

Ellie smiled, sensing the guilt in Elvie's voice. Her smile faded when she heard Elvie narrating again, her braille stylus punching, and recalled the tiny spot of taint she'd witnessed in her friend's life-glow, sitting between Elvie's eyes.

"Regardless of wot Helia learns, I've words with M'Lady Monocle," Ellie muttered and walked on to her room.

Elvie woke in the morning and felt as buoyant as a toy balloon. Mrs Darby remarked on her cheery disposition during breakfast, and Sarah enquired teasingly as to whether Elvie had met a potential beau at the marble-garden event. Elvie would neither confirm nor deny.

"Is Ellie here at the table?" Elvie asked instead.

Hearing that Ellie wasn't, but had come in late last night (and smelling of a fire's smoke), Elvie could forgive her for not returning to chaperone. But she intended to rouse her soon so Ellie could be present when Elvie visited the sculptress again. Gallivanting off to a public event with others in attendance had seemed harmless enough, but . . . .

A night of reflection made Elvie wonder how Lady Thanatou perceived her, especially when she sent a conveyance to fetch her. Elvie, though an independent woman, did not want to be viewed as "convenient." Uncertain if she was exaggerating circumstances, she put the concern away, finished her breakfast, then sought out fellow boarders who could care for her classes while she was out for the day.

In her room, Elvie fussed, nervous, and took inventory of her clays: her five *Aphrodites*, one *Laocoön*, a pregnant Mary (though fashioned like a pregnant, modern woman Elvie had once touched), one swaddled baby Jesus, three cats, one tortoise, two rabbits, one elephant (an admirable attempt based on zoo descriptions), three of her fellow boarders, Mrs Darby (who did not find the clay of herself flattering), and three different *fascina*.

Her mind returned, as it had all night and morning, to the sculptress. The mere thought of her made Elvie's heart quicken and her body lighten, as though gravity had been removed. She thought of the perfect hymn.

"'When Christ was born of pure Marie,'" she said. She
sang, changing the gender:

> Grant us, O Lady, for Thy great grace,
> In heaven in bliss to see Thy face,
> Where we may sing to Thy solace: *In excelsis gloria.*

> *In excelsis gloria!*
> *In excelsis gloria!*
> *In excelsis gloria!*
> Angels sang with mirth and glee,
> *In excelsis gloria!*

"Bold li'l elf, singin' of some lady instead of the Lord,"
Ellie said at the open doorway and walked in.

Elvie smiled sheepishly. "Good morning, Ellie. By now
you must have heard where I was yesterday."

"I 'ave, Elvie, 'n note my astonishment, when I told you
quite clearly to stay 'ome."

"They sent me a conveyance, Ellie. What was I to do?"

To her surprise, she felt Ellie touch her face, tilting it up
as if to study her features.

"You can tell me 'ow the visit went, that's what you can
do," Ellie said lightly. "Especially if you were treated well."

"Oh, I was!"

Elvie proceeded to tell her so, and listened to Ellie wander
about, as if by moving she could better mull upon Elvie's
words.

"And somehow, Ellie, she knew to send Ahmet, a person
to act as the world's *amanvensis*, and whose account I could
then later expatiate upon."

"Mm-hm," Ellie said.

"Lady Thanatou seems to understand that constant information is what stimulates my continued understanding of our world. Oh, Ellie! I'd like you both to meet—formally this time! So you won't think ill of her. I do think you'll like her."

"Sounds like you've made a friend, Elvie. More than a friend."

"Perhaps." Elvie rubbed at the pressure developing between her eye sockets, her enthusiasm suddenly diminished. "Already, I like her very much, but I am uncertain what such an interesting woman sees in me. She may be fond of me solely for my blindness. Like that fellow you had to end relations with, Ellie."

"Oh, that one. He liked 'airy women as well. And amputees. It's too early to say that about yer Lady Thanatou, Elvie."

"Well, Ellie, I'm just making myself aware in case it's so. I'm not so inclined to fend her off, regardless."

Elvie turned for her dresser top and readied a water glass. When she opened her drawer, she counted how many envelopes of headache powders she had left. "I must tell Mrs Darby to order more from the chemist," she muttered before she ingested one with water.

"Visit yer doctor instead, Elvie," Ellie said. "So that he may adjust your dosage and you can ingest that foul stuff less."

"I'm perfectly well, Ellie. I've no need to see him."

"You can easily afford the visit," Ellie said. "Especially as he's yer uncle. And yer surgeon."

"He keeps my childhood eyeballs in a jar. Is that not morbid? No, Ellie, I don't want to see him. He's certain to have invented yet another medical instrument to poke me in the eye sockets with and make me suffer, as I'm his most favourite test subject. Never mind him, what are your plans today, Ellie?"

"Well, I'm off to gallivant with that Helia Skycourt again. I'm needed to fend of 'er assassins, and that may take the entire day."

"Oh," Elvie said, unable to hide her disappointment. "The entire day?"

"What is it, Elvie? Have you need of an escort?"

"I—no, I shall be quite well. No, Ellie, I won't need an escort today. But please sit, I would like to ask you something."

She heard Ellie take a chair and sit down, and Elvie imagined Ellie as she'd once touched her. She knew there was a manner to Ellie's long, lean body, an attitude of form unique to her friend, and she'd wanted to capture it. Ellie had sat still at Elvie's instruction and Elvie touched her from head to toe: the tilt of her hat, the chin held high, the back and narrow shoulders erect, one arm crooked to rest her blackthorn, the other bent to place a firm hand on her hip. Ellie liked to cross her legs at the knee, her free foot kicking. That was how Elvie imagined Ellie whenever she sat down in her room. She'd made a clay of her in that position, and Ellie had thought it an apt likeness, though quite exaggerated.

"Ellie, you can sense the illness in a person. Or . . . just that they're wrong, like how Seward is a simpleton."

"Oh yes, Seward. I think he was dropped as a child."

"How do you know this taint, Ellie?"

"Hm." She heard Ellie's body shift. "Well, the taint, it's the wrong bit, Elvie. It's the bit in a person that ought not to be."

"But . . . what if someone were very different; perhaps something else entirely."

"That's not an affliction, Elvie. It'll feel very queer and we may have desire to kill it fer being so different, but that's our fearful selves speakin'. Now, I shall tell you something. When people talk of Africans 'n the Irish or the Jews. They measure the same to me as anybody: all as God made us. Then they open their mouths and speak or eat somethin' queer. That is merely dressin', for we're all the same meat when naked. Now, regarding the other sort, the ones unlike us. Often formed superior to us. You should meet them supernatural agents of the Secret Commission, Elvie. They're so different, it's like sensin' mighty elephants. If elephants could set themselves on fire or fly. Magical beings, one might say. And some can be dangerous, like lions amongst us lambs. Why do you ask, Elvie?"

"You've witnessed Lady Thanatou, Ellie. Then you must know."

"Yes, Elvie, she is quite different. Quite an elephant, she is."

At that Elvie smiled broadly. She could ask Ellie what sort of "different" but she was enamoured by the mystery of it. As Elvie mused on Lady Thanatou being a Greek woman, many possibilities came to mind. A fabled Amazon was one thought, for did the sculptress not intimidate the countess so effectively? A lioness, indeed. Buoyancy filled her, and she reached for her desk, found the surface, and pulled out the chair.

"I shall work more on my *ekphrases*," she said happily.

"Between you 'n Helia, I don't know what language I'm speakin'," Ellie said. "I take it that means you'll be busy for the day?"

"Oh yes, I've a great many descriptions to write of yesterday's marbles. Then I'll be teaching the newly blind the use of their slate and stylus."

"A busy day, then. I'll be 'appy to read yer ekfrah-sees later, especially those describing the male marbles' arbor vitaes."

Ellie rose, and Elvie laid out her metal braille slate, stylus, dictionary, and journal. She bade Ellie good day. But when she was certain Ellie had left the house, her blackthorn tapping the walk while Elvie listened at her room's window, she put her writings away, made herself presentable for going out, and then waited once more by her window. Soon she heard the clean, smooth hum of an electric vehicle's motor and rose, not bothering to wait for Mrs Darby to fetch her.

"Just this one more time," Elvie said with determination. "And—if her intentions are serious! Then I'll visit no more without a chaperone."

Satisfied by the decision, she descended.

CHAPTER EIGHT

Helia emerged from the late-morning bustle upon the walk and entered the lobby of Osbourne's in Westminster's Adelphi. After parting from Ellie and Annie yesterday, she'd gone to the hotel, returned the key she'd picked from Stravros's pocket, and learned he'd yet to return. She gave the desk clerk a shilling to notify her by messenger whenever Stravros should show his face, spent the evening typing away at her customary Blue Vanda table in the Royal Aquarium, then returned to Osbourne's to bribe the night clerk as well. Nothing came of it, and were she male she would have sat vigil in the lobby instead and worked on her various stories. But being a woman, she would have been taken for a loitering prostitute, even if banging away at typewriter keys. By late night and with still no word, she speculated that Stravros had found some other bed to sleep in.

Helia then visited Chelsea to look in upon Art and Atlas, locked in their continued wrestling match and watched by their partners, a few hardy spectators, and two sport journalists, the tense standstill lit by can fire and moonlight. Once she saw that Art was well, Helia resigned herself to a good night's sleep in her airship replica hanging in the aquarium.

Stavros had taken his hotel key with him instead of leaving it at the front desk, which seemed to Helia the action of an untrusting man, or one needing to hide his movements. She wondered what inspired his vendetta against Lady Thanatou, for he was too passionate to be a hired killer. As Ellie had noted, his lack of nerve in that regard was interesting as well.

"Hello," Helia said, smiling at the fresh-faced desk clerk who'd replaced the night one. "Can you tell me if Mr Stavros is still in, please?"

"Oh, him, well," the clerk said and smiled. He did not bother to look behind him at the bank of cubbyholes that held mail and hotel keys.

Helia mentally snorted; no doubt he thought her a prostitute. She held up a shilling.

"Make that three, miss, and I may tell you," he said.

Helia was about to retort when she spotted Stavros's dishevelled and wary figure in the mirrored wall beside the desk. She turned and confirmed; Stavros had entered the lobby, his right hand swollen and held close to his body. Helia pulled back her coin before the clerk could take it and moved to accost Stavros. He stopped at the sight of her.

"You," he ejected.

Helia paused in step and waved a hand before her face. Stavros's breath was foul with liquor and his body smelled of old sweat, but despite his bleary eyes he seemed more a man recovering than still drunk.

"Mr Stavros," she said. "Might I have a word? Concerning

Lady Thanatou."

"Deceived puppet," he snapped. "You are as blind as the rest of her followers."

Helia feigned surprise. "How so?"

"Why did you protect her, eh? Do you mask an illness that needs her promise as well, of some perfect, painless death?" Despite his fatigued state, his gaze held the fire of outrage. "You are a fool. She can give you death, yes, *or* life, but never the latter choice!"

"She can — save me? But how, Mr Stavros?" Helia urged. "Tell me."

His gaze narrowed. "How can you not — "

"I *am* ill, Mr Stavros," Helia interrupted. "And if I'm this *pharmakos* you mentioned to Mr Teegan, then I don't know what you know."

"Foolish sacrifice," he muttered, his gaze slipping away. Helia grabbed his arm.

"Tell me, Mr Stavros," she said.

He snatched his arm back. "Very well. Do you know what Athena of the flashing eyes gave the healer Asclepius? Two drops of the Gorgon's blood: one that healed and the other that killed. Drawn from the Gorgon's left side, her blood is poison, but drawn from the right, it *cured*." Stavros shook his swollen hand in emphasis. "Cured, understand? It can even resurrect the dead. My wife — my wife should be *alive*. Instead, she followed that creature and gave herself to the Gorgon!"

He leaned close, pinning Helia with his wild-eyed gaze. "That monster you foolishly follow is our *pharmakon*," he said, "the thing that is both our poison and remedy. She can *save* you and yet chooses not to."

The infection stirred behind Helia's mask, roiling at the

thoughts she suddenly entertained. She raised a trembling hand to the leather.

"Sh—shut it," she muttered in anger. Stavros looked at her in surprise. "But why do you want such a creature dead?" Helia then said. "When she could—"

"Never mind that." Stavros seized Helia's left wrist with his good hand, and before she could pull away, he stepped closer. "Are you *that* important to her?" he said, his tone deadly.

Helia breathed as he squeezed her wrist. She looked over his shoulder. Stavros noticed her gaze and looked as well. Ellie stood behind him, grinning at the space above his head. His angry gaze reflected in the black lenses of her spectacles.

"Perhaps yer other knuckles need a rappin'," Ellie suggested.

Stavros let go of Helia and stepped back, holding his swollen hand to himself. He backed farther away, glowering, then turned and walked on. Helia watched him accost the front desk's clerk and demand his room key.

When he left for upstairs, Helia rubbed her left wrist and turned to Ellie. "For that timely rescue, I shall buy you a coffee," she said.

⸻

"I had Elvie tell me of her visit, and she was treated well enough, though she could tell me naught about any magical eyes," Ellie said to Helia. They stood in the front room of Thackery Fine Dressmaker, Tailor, & Outfitter, on Robin Hood's Row in Cheapside, while Helia perused Charlotte Thackery's inventory of pocket mirrors. Ellie inspected the details of her own bodice front and found another minuscule croissant flake to brush off. Coffee with Helia could be quite a hoity-toit affair because she knew where a *pâtisserie* might be. Having missed breakfast at the Institute, Ellie was happy to stuff herself with sugar brioches and berry tarts whilst Helia muttered to herself and typed on her handheld typing contraption.

"Well, I witnessed her magical eye–its effects restrained behind glass, thankfully–hence my needing an appropriate polished shield to face Lady Thanatou with," Helia said as she discarded a choice made of imitation tortoise shell. The shop girl pulled out another tray for Helia to look at. "Since you were in too much haste to allow us to be properly outfitted yesterday, we shall be today."

"'N what did you learn from our Stavros? Anythin' that might outfit us?"

"He is an angry, angry man," Helia said. "Almost too much so."

She then related to Ellie the tale of the Gorgon's blood and the idea of the *pharmakon*, which Ellie thought nonsense, for even a ragged school student like herself knew blood moved all about the body. Therefore, blood, whether from the right or left side, was the same. She refrained from scoffing to forestall more fanciful tales.

"He did affirm Lady Thanatou as being that which we know her to be: the Gorgon. But he revealed something about her of even more concern."

"Wait, I have it," Ellie said. "Somethin' cultish."

"Oh? Annie thinks so too?"

"Well, you keep sayin' the woman's a 'goddess,' Helia. And so's that fellow in Rome, were he a woman. I believe our own queen's one to those who live a simpler livin'. If this Thanatou 'as girls followin' 'er about, I can't see 'ow it hurts anyone much, unless they like to perform them human sacrifices to 'er ladysh—" Ellie paused. "Oh."

"Yes. The *pharmakos*. One who is ill, a criminal, or, as you had said at Teegan's, Ellie, might be blind. We must find out," Helia said. She pocketed a silver hand mirror, then reached for something the shop girl brought over. She presented it to Ellie.

It was a thick mourning veil, worn all around and meant for freshly rendered widows who dared not peek beyond the curtains of their sorrow. Ellie's abilities could not sense the world through solid barriers, and the veil, when worn, was opaque and heavy enough to blind her like a bag over her head.

"Wot's this for?"

"For you to avoid petrifaction," Helia said.

"Is that like bein' made putrid?"

"No, Ellie, it's when you're made petrified."

"Humph." She wanted to toss the veil. "It's foolish to hood me. I may sense 'er exactly, Helia, but I can't gaze at 'er. I can't even know what's present in 'er eyeballs."

"Despite that lack of soul recognition, Ellie, we've no understanding of how *her* gaze works. Your unique perceptions might just be enough to fall into fascination. Would you rather be turned to stone to find out?"

"Me, turned to stone! Stuff 'n nonsense."

"'Nonsense' is an apt description for a blind woman with your senses," Helia retorted.

Ellie sighed and removed her hatpin, then her hat. She attached the veil to her chapeau, taking care not to muss her pheasant feathers, gathered all the fabric upon the brim, ready to be drawn down, then placed her hat back on her head.

"Oh, now we're suited up fine t'assail the beast," she said with sarcasm. "Out you go. With me followin' yer winged sandals."

———

Elvie descended to find Mrs Darby conversing with Corrina, and before Mrs Darby could query further about the day's outing, Elvie bade the housekeeper a hasty farewell and boarded the electric phaeton. Alexys drove her, Corrina, and Ahmet a short distance to where Elvie heard the rhythmic rush of waves, the creak of moored boats, and the constant clatter that was a bridge's traffic. Her first guess—and a correct one—as Alexys brought the phaeton to a halt was that they were beneath Queen Street Bridge.

When Corrina and Ahmet helped her disembark and step foot on the bankside pier, they introduced her to Lady Thanatou's surprise: a steam-powered pleasure boat, thirty-five feet long and lent by an acquaintance to be Elvie's water taxi. Having never ridden on the water before (for Ellie had a great distrust of water transports, whether wherries or modern steamboats), Elvie found the moored vessel, its constant motion, the lapping waters, and the idea of riding a body of water itself a giddy revelation. She attempted to walk the circumference of the rolling deck to gain a gist of the craft's shape, but after she nearly pitched herself over the railing, Corrina sat Elvie down in a deck chair on the bow, tucked a rug around her, and ordered the ship to leave. Elvie listened to the firetube's activation, heard the engine start and the ship's bell rung by the captain, felt the ship's propulsion beneath her feet, and held up her hands to catch the wind on her palms.

"We ride on top of water," Elvie marvelled, listening to

the river's water rapidly change shape along the prow.

"We are floating, miss," Corrina said. "Like a sponge we push along in the bath."

"We are sponges in the bath," Elvie said in wonderment, thinking that all the times she'd heard ships' engines or bells, or had the vessels described to her, she had not known that sailing had its own world, unique of experience and perception, until right then.

The first bridge they rode beneath was Blackfriars Bridge, and Ahmet delighted her by shouting so that the bottom of the bridge echoed back its height to her. She clapped her hands to cause directional echo as well, measuring the great distance above and to the sides for which taller and wider vessels needed to pass, and wondered if Sgt Trilby walked high above with his camera. But after passing under Waterloo Bridge and enjoying the echoes beneath it, Elvie fell into a state of reflection about her present experience, so generously gifted to her by the sculptress. It was more than a doting gesture.

I've been acting the schoolgirl and not taking her fondness seriously, she thought.

"Miss, does something concern you?" Corrina asked.

"I was thinking of how my friend Miss Hench was unavailable to come, Corrina," Elvie said. "And now I feel remiss in acquiring company for this outing."

"Oh, miss, I hope I and our lady's attendants may prove adequate company to you."

"Yes, but you serve Lady Thanatou, Corrina," she said. "And that's not quite like being chaperoned."

Ahmet suddenly distracted her by declaring their approach to Westminster Bridge, and Elvie forgot to ponder whether Corrina understood her need.

Their short journey down the Thames soon ended, and when their boat docked in Chelsea's Cremorne Pier and its pleasure garden, Alexys and the electric phaeton awaited them. From there to Brompton hamlet the travel seemed no time at all, and despite entry into idyllic surroundings, the fluttering of Elvie's stomach grew. She wanted to emulate Ellie and handle the visit like an independent woman would, but it would also be her first time spent alone with someone who was not well known to her. The sculptress was a sort of elephant, after all.

After the phaeton had come to a stop and Ahmet and Corrina had helped her out, she heard two sets of approaching feet on the driveway's gravel. But one pair she knew—the feet touched the gravel lighter than the rest, the steps measured and deliberate. Elvie smelled pungent roses and could not help smiling broadly.

"*Hypíaine*, Elvie," the sculptress said, and Elvie thought her tone both welcoming and pleased. Before she could answer and thank her for the boat ride, she felt Corrina step away and heard her whisper in Greek, swift and urgent. She was about to ask what was the matter when the furtive discussion stopped.

"Elvie," the sculptress said. "I do not believe you have met Mrs Nothings—"

"Nottings," Adara murmured.

"Yes. She was here for the event of *haphê* and is presently enjoying tea within. You desire a chaperone for your visit, do you not?"

"Why, I do," Elvie said, suddenly glad.

"*Kala*. She will remain during the entirety of your visit and be your chaperone. Come." At the request, Elvie reached out and felt the sculptress take her hands, then lead Elvie into the crook of her arm. She grasped the roughened hand of that arm and settled close to the lady's side.

Oh, she is warm, Elvie thought, inhaling her perfume.

"Miss," Adara said. "Would you like Mrs Nottings to leave her tea and accompany you?"

"Oh, Adara, she needn't do that," Elvie said, feeling self-conscious.

"Then this way to my studio, Elvie," the sculptress beckoned, and at her low tone, Elvie complied. Lady Thanatou walked her up the steps of the portico and into her home.

CHAPTER NINE

"Was the boat ride to your liking?" the sculptress asked.

"It was wonderful! Life on the water is a whole other world, and I would have never known it. Thank you for showing it to me," Elvie said.

"It was my pleasure to give you the experience. There is more beneath the waters, as well," the sculptress said. "Though better experienced in purer seas."

"Such as?" Elvie asked, curious.

"Poseiden's realm," the lady simply answered.

Elvie would have queried more but felt again the brief intervals of sun within the vestibule, and when she raised her face to feel the warmth, the sculptress told her of the skylights above, allowing the rays of Helios in. She also mentioned the distinct decorations and themes of the rooms they passed, where ancient Greek tales were told on the walls as frescoes, and more lay on the floor as mosaics.

"And did you create all those as well?" Elvie asked.

"Do you think me so accomplished?" the sculptress said, her tone wry.

"With hands like these, yes," Elvie answered, grasping the one that led her.

They progressed thus in alternating shadow and light, the sculptress then enquiring how Elvie had spent her night. Elvie told her of her mundane night activities. But she did wonder what the lady meant by the question, for it sounded quite like innuendo. She was aware right then, being so close to the sculptress, of the power harboured in a body that was so deceptively womanly. It was like the latent strength she'd perceived when hugging a Shire horse, greater than any ordinary human's. And Elvie knew the sculptress had a womanly body, for Ellie had described it so, though Elvie wouldn't mind affirming the description with her own hands.

"I am pleased you are here, Elvie," Lady Thanatou said as Elvie felt and heard their entry into the peristyle garden's portico. "Had I not fled after my . . . communication to you, at the museum, this would have been the natural progression of our meeting."

"You seem hardly the sort that flees," Elvie said, bemused.

"You had an intimidating companion with you at the time, had you not?"

"Ellie certainly is that." *Though not to one like you.* "And perhaps I wouldn't have been so quick to call for her if not for—well, never mind, I speak of a resolved matter. Why were you in Room 84 of the British Museum, if I might ask? I don't believe the antiquities there are worth your scrutiny."

"Tell me why you were there, little *kore*," the sculptress said.

"I am not a *kore*. It's the sole place I might touch them, the sculptures. I'm now watched very carefully in the other galleries, especially after exploring the colossal nostrils of Amenotep III."

She noted the pause from her companion that often

signalled the suppression of a reaction: a chuckle, a gasp, an exasperated sigh. When the sculptress finally spoke, Elvie thought she heard humour in the tone.

"I visit as a reminder, Elvie, of what I should not do."

"I understand. When I touch those mediocre marbles, I am inspired to endeavour with my clays. Though my manner of expression might be considered naively earnest."

"You sculpt as well?"

"If a modeller is a sculptor, then yes," Elvie murmured, suddenly shy.

"You are a lover of the contour," the sculptress said, her voice low. "Of the forms made with hands. As am I."

Elvie's breath quickened. The lady came to a stop. A wind chime tinkled nearby.

"My studio," the sculptress said, and she led Elvie into a doorway from which she smelled the sharp scent of fresh dust, made from stone rent asunder.

Elvie paused at the threshold, gripped the sculptress's arm, and her companion paused. She raised her free hand and performed a trick she and other blind had been discouraged from using for its impropriety: she snapped her fingers hard.

Snap.

She heard the echo's reverberation within the room, giving her the presence of far walls. She lowered her hand and snapped again, the echo indicating that the floor was lower than where she stood.

Overcome with excitement, she said nothing but only patted Lady Thanatou's arm. Elvie felt her let go, one hand upon her, and step down. Elvie was wondering why she'd been left behind when the sculptress placed her hands at her waist. She did not lift but waited.

"Yes," Elvie said, and the sculptress brought her up like a

mere balloon. For half a second, Elvie flew. She contacted concrete and heard the echo of her landing.

She was aware of big things in the room; the echoes of her finger snaps marked their presence but once on the floor she didn't know where the objects lay. More snaps would tell her, but instead she wanted the sculptress to describe the contents of her workplace. They wandered the floor, swept clean of debris and dust, while the sculptress explained the commissions she was working on and the sculpting process, for not all of her work, she said, was rendered in marble. Methods like plaster casting, moulds, lost-wax casting, and sand casting had Elvie's mind reeling. The lady spoke with quiet evenness, but her tone held an underlining passion and earnestness Elvie could not help sharing in. Though she had nothing but a layman's appreciation for the final product of such a complicated process, Elvie hoped she might soon comprehend the entirety of the art known as sculpting.

Thus informed, she explored a partially chiselled stone from whose roughness a woman emerged. She ran her hands along a male's hewn body where so many bites of the toothed chisel needed the rasp applied to remove the marks. She touched another female in its final stage of smoothing, positioned beneath a water fixture mounted in the ceiling to aid in its wet sanding. Elvie thought the entire room energised with possibility, its creative fervour slumbering until vigour and cacophony resumed again.

"I do not perform all the work myself," the sculptress admitted. "My apprentices, who also serve my house as attendants, may carve under my direction. And there are the students who pay to learn. They are very useful for the final polishing and sealing of the pieces. I will also have pieces cast in bronze, but I prefer those done with a French foundry."

"You are prolific," Elvie exclaimed. "Tireless."

"I am merely a skilled carver, a *practicien*," the sculptress said. "I will still render copies for buyers."

"You are an artist," Elvie said, emphatic. "I thought Thana exceptional."

"Thank you," the sculptress murmured. With her palm at the small of Elvie's back, she gave Elvie's fingers a light tug and manoeuvred her around what Elvie assumed was another obstacle, for there were many of those in the studio.

How easily you lead me, Elvie thought, and she wondered: was such assured guidance like "dancing"?

"Now; here are laid the small stones I work on when feeling idle. Move freely and touch, Elvie, for all obstructions and sharp things have been removed for you."

The worktable the sculptress placed her before came above Elvie's waist. Elvie reached and contacted a figurine, so small it fit in her palm. Then she slowly swept her hands around to comprehend the entire table and brushed more stone figures of different sizes and rotundity. But all the figurines shared the same generous body traits: they were well-endowed, prehistoric Venuses.

"More little ones!" Elvie exclaimed, delighted. "And so fecund." She laughed.

She encountered no chairs to bump into and nothing on the table she might knock over as she sought to touch all the dear small sculptures, each of a different weight and feel that seemed to indicate a different material, and which she asked the sculptress to identify. Bone, ivory, limestone, calcite — she tried to learn them all. She soon realised that she'd not heard the lady reply for a while, though Elvie exclaimed her discoveries to her.

"Lady Thanatou?" she said.

"You are like a newborn foal dancing in a meadow," the sculptress said, her voice warm.

"Oh, what does that mean," Elvie said, "to dance? I would not understand a foal running, either, though I've heard people running."

"On a beach, you, your own body and legs, may run forever," the sculptress said, "fall safely upon the sand, and get up again. You will learn." She touched Elvie and Elvie turned to her, lured by the heat from the sculptress's proximity.

"But come," she said before Elvie could ask what she meant. "Something awaits your touch."

⁓

The sculptress led her to an area with tall windows, for the sun's warmth touched Elvie's face. At her prompting, Elvie reached and contacted a broad back. She felt along the bending spine of a great man that dwarfed her.

"How muscular," she said in awe.

"It is a marble of Ajax, son of Telamon and Periboea, whom the English know as Ajax Telamonius. This *Ajax* is my copy of what remains of the Roman copy."

"I know that name, Ajax Telamonius, he was one of the Greek heroes in Homer's *Iliad*." Elvie reached up on tiptoe and swept her arms all about the bent back of the figure, trying to feel the whole of him. "He is massive."

"He is." The sculptress's voice came from the other side of the marble, and when she spoke, Elvie noted the slow travel of her voice.

She is circling, she thought as she touched the *Ajax*.

"Ajax was colossal of frame, a giant among men," the sculptress said, her voice to Elvie's right. "Courageous, mighty, and peerless in battle, with only Achilles his superior. Great were his deeds during the Trojan War, but compared to Odysseus, he seemed a man lacking tongue and intelligence. When he lost the prize of Achilles's armour to Odysseus, Ajax went mad, aggrieved by injustice and his own bitter disappointment."

"This is he, in despair," Elvie said, reaching for his shoulders.

"It is." The sculptress passed her left side. "Sophocles told that Ajax's madness was given him by the gods, driving him to slaughter a herd of sheep who he thought were his own comrades."

"He meant to kill . . . his own men?"

"In madness, he did. Once sane, his shame caused him to fall upon the sword that was Hector's gift to him, and from his spilt blood a red flower sprang. On the leaves were his initials, AI, which for we Greeks, is the sound of lament."

"Such a sad story."

"It is a common story, Elvie."

Elvie listened and marked the sculptress again on the marble's other side, still moving.

"In Greek tragedies, yes," Elvie said, knowing the sculptress passed to her right.

"And today," the sculptress said, low, behind her. "Women, in deep shame or grief, still choose such a fate."

Sobered, Elvie touched where arms, head, and legs would be, finding all missing. She felt along the breaks and noted their softening by sanding, as if to imitate the passage of time on their once-sharp, hurtful edges. All the while, she felt the silent, roaming sculptress's attention on her, like the regard of a hundred eyes.

If a gaze could be a touch, she thought.

"Yet your *Ajax* is broken," Elvie said. "Very broken."

"The original is so. It has lost its head, arms, and legs. Thus I broke mine."

"But . . . you cannot break it without first—" Elvie paused her hands. "You know what the true *Ajax* looked like?" she said, incredulous.

The sculptress did not answer, and Elvie regretted her tone.

"You guessed at what the *Ajax* might have looked like," she clarified.

"Of course," the lady softly answered, once again on the other side.

"Yet you broke yours, though it could have remained intact, perfect. Beautiful." Elvie searched about the pelvis, finding the penis had also not survived. "This, your recreation, could have given us the majesty of the whole pose. A tragic pose."

"But wholeness is not the truth," the sculptress said, her voice nearing. "It is not the reality of the *Ajax*. He was damaged and this is all that survived. Cannot beauty be found in what remains?"

Elvie moved around the *Ajax* and felt the sculptress follow.

"Help me touch, please," she said, raising her arms for the statue's back.

The lady understood. She came behind and lifted her up, and Elvie reached around and embraced the giant, feeling in the remnants of the bent figure, its eternal anguish and sorrow.

"Yes," she finally answered.

When the sculptress let her down, Elvie had a request.

"Might I handle your tools?" she asked.

"My tools?" The sculptress said, her tone surprised. "It would . . . *please* me to have you know them, yes." Elvie thought she nearly purred the word. "But I have something better prepared for you."

"Oh?" Elvie said.

"I will now show you how to carve."

Elvie clapped hands over her mouth, suppressing her shout of delight. Lady Thanatou led her to another tall tabletop where she gently removed Elvie's hands from her mouth and placed them on a stone surface higher than the tabletop. Elvie felt up and down the block, finding it big enough to carve a bust.

"What sort of material is it?" she asked, eager.

"It is soapstone, Elvie, very soft and easy to carve, and set on a bag of sand to absorb the vibrations of your blows. It is a small block, and therefore perfect for you." The sculptress's tone sounded indulgent, and Elvie wanted to question if she thought her so delicate. "It is best to carve using your entire body, but you are just beginning."

"And I am blind," Elvie said. "I understand. We blind move with less assurance and bodily awareness than the sighted." She heard and felt a tall stool placed at her backside.

"You will learn more about your own body soon," the lady said, helping her up, and Elvie wondered at her light tone, implicit with meaning. "*Kala*. Now . . . here is your mallet, and your point chisel. I will help you strike the block, and then you will feel what the first step of shaping is like."

"Oh," Elvie exclaimed as she felt all around the mallet, then the chisel. The sculptress came behind her, bending down, and reached around her body. Elvie would have been distracted by her closeness if not for her fascination with the tools.

"Careful of the sharp edge, Elvie," the sculptress said softly near her ear. "Hold your chisel so . . . and the mallet so. We place the chisel's point at an angle. Like this. And we raise the mallet . . . ." She raised Elvie's arm. But once Elvie's hand left the table, she did not know where she was in space and air.

"I have never—I don't know the motion," Elvie said, frustrated.

The sculptress held each of her hands in her own. "Raise it so, Elvie," she repeated, close to her ear, and adjusted her arm. Her breath tickled and Elvie squirmed.

"I—no—I need to feel it. It's not just in the hands, is it? If you sit behind me, then I'll know it from your body."

Lady Thanatou paused, then urged Elvie off the stool. It scraped as the sculptress sat down, and when she coaxed Elvie to sit again by lifting her up, she found enough room between the lady's legs to perch comfortably. Elvie moved back more and felt the sculptress's bosom against her back. Heat and the scent of roses embraced her, and gripping the tools in each hand, she exhaled in happiness.

"Do you know how people would say, to 'behold'?" she remarked. "I've been told it means to be held in one's gaze. Transfixed." She paused, pondering the word. "I feel that is what we are presently doing. My arms are your arms, or your arms are mine. I can know you by your body, for we fit now. I behold you."

"That is *haptesthai*, Elvie," the sculptress whispered, and Elvie took a breath, her heart hammering. The weight the lady gave the word seemed to imply more than just "to touch." She attempted to bring her hands up. The sculptress guided them; she held Elvie's hands and repositioned the chisel against the stone at an angle, then raised the mallet. Elvie pressed her raised arm against Lady Thanatou's, the limb strong yet yielding, and found the form of the action. Her arms were, right then, the sculptress's arms.

"Show me," Elvie softly demanded.

The lady did so, moving Elvie's body in slow practice first, familiarising her with the entire act of bringing her mallet down upon the head of the chisel. Then she swung Elvie's arm down.

Elvie struck a blow that she felt in her fist and in the hand that slipped away with the chisel. The abrupt detachment of the shorn stone made her squeal, and she put the tools down to search for her chip. Finding it, she touched all around the piece to explore what she had created. It was a new, little thing, and with the strength of the sculptress— for she couldn't deny it was her power that had done the deed—Elvie had carved change into the block. She put the chip in her pocket and then clapped her hands. The lady laughed behind her, the mirth held in her chest and throat, and Elvie could not help herself; she pressed back against the moving bosom to feel the sound.

"Oh, now what is it?" Elvie said, pretending to be peeved.

"You are like the squirrel, hiding a nut," the sculptress said.

"Unlike the squirrel, I don't intend to eat my chip," Elvie said, and realising that the sculptress steadied her at the waist with both hands, she reached down and soothed the backs to soften her words. She felt the prominent veins and revelled in their lines. Her touch ran up beneath the cuffs, wanting more.

Something hissed. Elvie stiffened, and one of the

sculptress's hands slipped from hers. The mallet clattered on the table, startling her, and she wondered how and when it had been lifted. The sculptress picked Elvie up by the waist and set her on her feet.

"I—I am a poppet in your hands," Elvie said, her brief laugh shaky. She listened, thinking the hiss might have come from a hot water pipe overhead. She heard nothing more and then became aware of the vacancy behind her.

Lady Thanatou had withdrawn. Elvie did not feel her near, in heat or scent, and decided not to dwell on why the sculptress had chosen to distance herself right then. Elvie herself needed to regain her own composure and breathed to slow the beat of her heart. She reached for the block of soapstone.

"Careful, Elvie," the lady cautioned, and Elvie thought she sounded several paces away, perhaps even across the room. Elvie smiled as she felt the block beneath her hands and found the spot where the shaping had begun.

"Wonderful stone, what will you be?" she said, feeling the whole of it. "What hides within you? Whatever the outcome, you will be beautiful."

She listened. She smelled roses first before noting the slight brush of fabric right behind her. The sculptress touched Elvie's elbow.

"Come. That is enough for today."

⌐

They left the studio, and Elvie enjoyed a brief stroll through the marble garden while on the sculptress's arm, delighting in the warmth of sun and the beguiling scent of her companion. She did not want to detach even to explore more sculptures, though she did answer Lady Thanatou's question of what she had enjoyed touching during her last visit.

"The *Kallipygos* is so appropriately named," Elvie said with admiration. "I must reproduce her attributes next in my clays."

"Was her form so pleasing to you?" the sculptress asked, the question purred. Elvie thought Lady Thanatou's tone seemed self-satisfied.

"Oh, very. How I wish I knew more modern works like yours. The idea of further experiencing examples of the classical ideal has become staid to my hands."

"Are you familiar with the work of Sarah Bernhardt?" the lady said. "Besides acting, she is an accomplished *sculpteur*. You would enjoy her *Death of Ophelia.*"

"I am only familiar with the works in Room 84," Elvie said. "Your work, your garden, has given me more than I could ever dream of our world. I am grateful for all that you've allowed me to touch and know, especially Thana. She is so beautiful."

"She is my most favourite work, my memory," the sculptress said in a soft tone.

Elvie nearly asked if the sculptress had meant "memorial."

"What happened to Thana?" she said instead.

"She became ill," the lady said. "Very ill, and nothing helped."

They entered the house, and Elvie wondered how fresh Lady Thanatou's suffering might be.

Corrina welcomed them into the triclinium, their dining room, and the lady seated Elvie for what she called *hesperisma*: a light meal of bread, grapes, olives, figs, cheese, smoked eel, and braised mushrooms. Corrina arranged Elvie's plate, explaining where each item was according to a clock's face, and encouraged her to use her hands. When Elvie learned that the sculptress ate with her fingers as well, she wholeheartedly did so. Someone played a stringed instrument described to her as a lyre, and a table fountain gurgled. If Mrs Nottings was still present in the house, Lady Thanatou either forgot or had no inclination to invite the woman to join them, and Elvie, too, pretended to forget. The sculptress, despite her overt interest in her, seemed committed to being a gentlewoman. Or, Elvie thought, she was just being patient.

"I think it very convenient to eat with one's hands," Elvie said, finding a cut fig on her plate. "We boarders at the Institute would do so more at the table if Mrs Darby didn't listen for the sounds of our cutlery." She ate the fig and enjoyed its succulent, sweet flesh.

"We are presently eating in the manner of Greeks," the lady said, and Elvie thought her tone relaxed. She did not dine with Elvie at her table but was reclined, she had said, on a couch near her. Elvie was uncertain how the sculptress managed such a position in a corset, but she did not sound at all discomfited.

"Is it also the manner of Greeks to have a bathing room?" Elvie asked. "It seems like something physical culturists would favour." She found her smoked eel and bread and ate of both.

"Do you visit your English bathhouses, Elvie?"

"Oh no, though I'd love to. We blind don't know what to do in a pool. Except perhaps drown."

"That is morbid, Elvie."

"I know. But there is much that can morbidly happen to us in this world. Like surprise ditches, angry animals, or careless carriages. I dislike oblivious kerbs."

"There are no kerbs inside my bathing room," the sculptress said.

"Ours has a heated pool, miss, with circulating waters," Corrina said, replenishing Elvie's plate. Elvie felt around its clock face and found more cheese and olives. "One may also enjoy a steam bath and reinvigorate in the cold pool."

"What a wonderful home," Elvie enthused. "And you've an aviary and conservatory! It takes time for one like myself to learn a house's entirety. And even then I can only know it by a room, a hall, or a stair, one at a time."

"You are an adventuress, Elvie," Lady Thanatou said, and Elvie heard and smelled wine poured into a metal vessel.

"I do like to explore, though one must warn me of any ditches. And I suppose I take so long to learn a shape and place because I value precision. I like the truth about things and not merely their impressions."

She took in the sound of the sculptress drinking. When she spoke, her tone was pensive.

"But there is poetry in impressions, Elvie."

"You are correct. What are my clays, if not exaggerations? But to be able to move with freedom in our world, I need the truth of it. Then I'll be present, connected. I'll be cognisant; especially of you."

Elvie listened and knew she had the sculptress's attention.

"I have yet to know the measure of your entire studio, of your garden. But do you know how I could?"

"How?" the sculptress asked, her soft tone indulgent.

"If it were to rain, inside your studio and in your garden, I would know the surfaces and distances of everything, for each striking raindrop would tell me them. Continuously, on and on, water would fall and coat the world, rendering it entirely aural, and I would hear your tools, the stone, the wood, your garden, and know the placement of all things."

Elvie raised her hands, imagining the touch of rain right then.

"I could even find you," she said.

⌇

After the meal, Corrina bathed Elvie's hands in a bowl and dried them. Elvie heard the plates cleared and tried her best to mark the sculptress's location, at least by scent, for the sound of her movements still eluded her. She heard Adara speak in low tones to someone, mentioning another visitor, and she wondered if Lady Thanatou was with Adara. Her olfactory sense became overwhelmed by the smell of roses and frankincense when the lady came behind her.

"You must come again," the sculptress said, her voice low.

"Yes." Elvie did not turn around. If she did, she might end up in the sculptress's arms. "And this time I'll secure my escort."

"We know each other more and more; what need have you for a chaperone?" the lady said lightly.

"Must you disregard propriety?" Elvie said, and her cheeks grew hot. "But I should expect that of you. You were quite forward already, when you communicated to me at the museum."

"I was," the sculptress said, her tone smug.

You are the cat that ate the cream, Elvie thought. She turned. "Come visit me," she said, and when the sculptress did not answer, she hurried on. "I'm not as skilled as you. Hardly of any measure. But I'd like you to view my own attempt at figures. My clays. Won't you come to the Institute of the Blind and experience them?"

"You surprise me," Lady Thanatou said.

"How so?" Elvie asked.

"You surprise me by surprising me often," the lady said, her tone warm. "Are all at your institute like you?"

"Oh, I don't know. I'm merely myself, Elvie," she said with a smile.

"I will come," the sculptress answered.

Tomorrow, she promised Elvie, the word echoing in her mind as Corrina ushered her away, and Elvie's senses became bereft of heat and roses. She nearly didn't mind being swept thus from the presence of Lady Thanatou like some object needing putting away. If she had remained longer, she might have risked leaning closer and thus initiated a kiss.

She boarded the phaeton, flustered, a little bewildered, and not yet ready to resign herself to the sheer giddiness inspired by thoughts of the sculptress. She barely noticed Adara instructing Ahmet to remain or that a horse snorted nearby on the drive, indicating the presence of another carriage. They drove away, Corrina still tucking a rug about her. Elvie reached beneath to feel within her dress pocket, for in it was the sculptress's gift, a Venus Elvie had chosen from the worktable. It was of simple soapstone, but Elvie had delighted in the polished shape, all of round surfaces, the entire object feeling the softest of its sisters. The most prominent mark upon its body was the sharp incision indicating its tiny vulva.

She brought it out and kissed its little head, and did not pay heed to the sounds of yet another approaching carriage.

CHAPTER TEN

Helia watched as their carriage passed the Hoop and Toy and hoped their visit with Lady Thanatou would end civilly. She wouldn't mind stopping later at the pub for a rump-steak pudding. She turned to look at Ellie, who sat before her, hands resting on her blackthorn, and chin raised, as if regarding the carriage ceiling. The veil she'd insisted her friend wear lay piled at the ready atop her hat's brim. Though Ellie grinned like one who found life pleasant or even amusing, Helia knew it was her way of deflecting attention while she waited, patient as a cobra, for the right moment to strike.

"That Stavros," Ellie suddenly said. "I'm certain he'll try for Lady Thanatou again. When he's ready. His wife's turned to rock, I do understand, but I still didn't like the make of 'im. His anger was hot enough for me to measure."

"Well, Ellie, I will admit, I was glad to confront him in a public place. I might have been battered otherwise."

"I'm glad as well, Helia. Had he battered you, it would be more than 'is knuckles I'd be rappin'. That man will see 'imself stuck upon a vengeful shiv one night."

"Such anger, it is like from a man who has lost everything."

"Him, lose everything? That paralysis that possessed you and Helene when Art first died. *That* is loss, Helia."

Helia nodded, sober.

"No, instead of grievin', Stravros kicks things. He has quite the dislike of our monocled lady, and it seems with good reason, considering 'ow many women have gone on to their everlasting, stony eternity thanks to 'er. I might be made a wee bit angry were I to fail Elvie. And that would not be inspired by my loss, Helia, as much by my 'umiliation."

Helia nodded again, wondering if Ellie had ever pursued someone with the purpose of killing them. The injuries Ellie meted out with her stick were effective enough to end men long after an encounter with her.

"You would be more patient," Helia said.

"Well, I'd just be quieter in going about it."

<hr />

The horse clopped, the carriage rolled, and Ellie sensed nature as far as she could reach in the fluid world. It wasn't like being in a park or arboretum. Homes, gardens, nurseries, and other structures merged and emerged from the greenery that Ellie did not know as "green" but as living things. Southwark was pleasant to live in, relatively safe and peaceful, but Brompton was another sort of peace. It was prettier, at times untidier, and still wild enough to hide satyrs and elves. She recalled a fitting word.

"Bucolic," she said.

"Very," Helia agreed. "And most umbrageous."

"Humph," Ellie said.

She heard the whir of wheels and sensed female cyclists, pedalling like mad, coming abreast of the carriage. In single file, they sped past and down the avenue.

"Women racers," Helia scoffed. "Rude of them to ban me from the Wheel Club. As the superior cyclist, I can't help but win their silly competitions."

"This Brompton hamlet," Ellie said. "I've never had reason to visit. It's very quiet. Very sleepy."

"Not a bit of trouble to be found here, I'm certain," Helia said drily. Their carriage turned. "Here's our address. Oh my! That must be Lady Thanatou's, that lovely horseless phaeton."

Ellie cast her reading of the fluid world beyond their slowing carriage and witnessed the humming phaeton Helia spoke of. As it accelerated by them on the drive, she marked the facial surfaces of the passenger within that distinctly identified Elvie, her face upturned and smiling.

"Why that li'l minx!" Ellie said.

"Ellie?"

"Our Lady of the Monocle moves swiftly in 'er courtin'," Ellie muttered. "She sent a conveyance for Elvie again, and of course she accepted!"

"The blind girl in the phaeton, of course. Miss Chaisty didn't look harmed, Ellie."

"Neither was Eve when speakin' to 'er serpent in the garden," Ellie replied, and once the carriage came to a stop, promptly disembarked while Helia instructed their driver to wait.

The first things Ellie noted upon approaching the home of Lady Thanatou were the presence of another waiting carriage, the locations of the entrance and windows, how many storeys the house had, and the lone, living presence within the scope of her reading: a large footman at the portico. She tapped her blackthorn as she and Helia walked and narrowed her awareness upon the man, searching him for the shapes of concealed weapons. He suddenly turned, entered the house, and shut the doors behind him. She and Helia came to a stop at the bottom of the portico steps.

"Hm," Ellie said.

"Ellie, did you smile most menacingly again?"

"I did not, Helia. It were yer mad grin that scared 'im."

The doors opened. A woman stood at the entrance and looked down coldly.

"I am Adara, keeper of this house. What business have you at the house of Thanatou?" she demanded.

Helia stepped near, smiling, and presented her card. Ellie fished in her pocket and then offered one of her own.

"Might I introduce myself and my colleague? I am Helia Skycourt, journalist for the *Times*, and this is Miss Ellie Hench. We must speak to your mistress, Lady Thanatou, on a concern of the utmost importance."

"Shatterer!" Adara accused. "Destroyer! Nuisance!"

Ellie stood stock-still in surprise. She studied the direction of the woman's regard and decided Adara was addressing her and not Helia.

"Miss, I don't even know you," Ellie said.

Helia succeeded in getting Adara to accept her card, then straightened with a smile.

"How very astute, madame! She is correct, Ellie," Helia said. "You do like to break things."

"I 'aven't broken one sculpted object. Ask the British Museum," Ellie said, offended.

"You are referring to her stick, I believe?" Helia asked

Adara. "What if she were to leave it with you?"

"Come," Adara merely said and turned to move back inside the house. Helia looked at Ellie with a raised eyebrow, walked quickly up the steps, and entered. Ellie squared her shoulders and followed.

"Lovely statue. Lovely urn," Ellie said, referring to the antiquities sitting within hall niches as they walked. She could not sense the large footman anywhere, but heard tinkling wind chimes and became aware of an open-air courtyard, at hall's end, beyond whose columns lay greenery. Before Ellie could measure the scope of the fluid-entirety before her, the housekeeper paused before an airy sitting room, its veranda doors flung open. Within, two female servants were laying tea.

"You may come with me," Adara said to Helia. She turned to Ellie and held out her hand for her stick. "But Miss Hench must stay here."

"I, stay 'ere?" Ellie said, disbelieving. "You don't know who yer lettin' in, miss."

"Ellie," Helia hissed.

"We *know*," Adara said. She waited. Ellie sighed and handed her blackthorn over. The tea, at least, with its tiers of sweets, cakes, and savoury sandwiches, appeared quite delectable, and Ellie didn't mind investigating it.

"Remember my concern, Helia," Ellie said as she sauntered in. "Don't get distracted."

"I won't, Ellie," Helia assured, and Ellie sat in the chair a servant pulled out for her.

<hr>

The housekeeper gave Ellie's stick to another servant who stood by, then turned to Helia.

"Follow me, please."

Helia did, peering into sunlit cubiculums with blue-and-red wall frescos, colourful floor mosaics, and elegant, modern furnishings. Birds twittered in the distance, accompanied by the soft ringing of wind chimes. Somewhere, a fountain flowed. Above, she saw the red arches of gallerys within the vestibulum and the blue-rimmed skylights, allowing sunlight in. Her breath caught; were it possible to step back into a time two thousand years past, her present surroundings might be evidence of such a way of life, no longer known. Adara led her out of the vestibulum and past Ionic columns surrounding a central, open-air courtyard— the peristylium—in which a marble garden lay. Helia stepped within the sunlit place and marvelled at the figures, thinking them not just beautiful in form and shape but striking in their sensuality.

"I thought one was meant to be blindfolded to visit here," Helia said.

Adara said nothing and brought her before a nude, female marble that stood in the garden's centre. Chiselled manacles hung from the statue's wrists.

"*The Slave*," Helia whispered.

"Wait here, please," Adara said and departed.

Helia looked upon the marble maiden's face, its shadowed visage touched by sorrow.

"Dear Rose," she said.

A man's angry voice broke the quiet. Helia stepped away from the marble of Rose Batts and saw Tiberius Teegan emerge from the portico and into the garden's end, his tall form belligerent. Helia stepped again to look around another marble, wondering whom he addressed. Lady Thanatou stood in purple and black, head cocked and golden mask gleaming in the sunlight. The lady regarded Teegan through her monocle as if he were a small, yapping dog.

"What is this about a cure, that—that you are a *pharmakon?*" he shouted. "Is it true you could have saved my Dolly?"

Both Adara and the large footman approached him. But Teegan started away and moved for Lady Thanatou.

"Answer me!" he cried.

What happened next seemed a blur to Helia; he grabbed for Lady Thanatou, yet stumbled, and in the moment of the lady catching him, he managed to connect the palm of his hand with her face. Her golden mask fell aside.

Adara turned and covered her eyes. The footman did the same. Helia spun around and pressed against the statue at her back.

Mirror, mirror! she thought, heart pounding. She pulled it out and in her shaky grasp, it flashed repeatedly in the sunlight. She held it up.

Teegan stood, mouth agape and his body off-kilter, as if frozen in midstruggle. He was no longer a man but all of white stone, his blank eyes staring. Helia adjusted her mirror to find Lady Thanatou and had a moment of fright.

No! Perseus used a polished surface! I won't turn to stone, she reassured herself, even as her heartbeat sped. The unsteady reflection revealed a part of Lady Thanatou with her hand raised to her face, reaffixing her gleaming mask.

"Adara," the lady said.

Adara turned and dropped her hands, and the footman did the same. Then Thanatou removed the metal syringe from its casing and stepped to the paralysed Teegan. She sank the needle into his neck and compressed the syringe. Helia moved her mirror again to watch Teegan.

Beneath the bright sunlight, colour crept back into Teegan's surfaces: his silvered hair, the paled skin, the black of his mourning suit. His face, body, and clothes softened, and his eyelids shut. A sound escaped his parted lips, both a painful exhale and desperate moan. He collapsed and the footman caught him.

Helia turned her mirror and watched Lady Thanatou snap the syringe back into its case.

The syringe—it contains a restorative, Helia thought, amazed.

"Ahmet, see that he receives care," Adara ordered. Ahmet placed the fainted Teegan on his shoulders and carried him away. Then Helia noticed that Lady Thanatou stared in her direction. Adara also stared into Helia's mirror.

Helia put the mirror away. She tucked a stray curl into her hat, straightened her bodice, and then stepped away from the statue shielding her. Since neither Lady Thanatou nor Adara moved, Helia walked the length of the garden to where Lady Thanatou stood. Each step brought her closer to a bright, blue eye that glared behind the monocle. Helia came to a stop.

"The healer Asclepius was given two drops of the Gorgon's blood," she said, trying to still the nervous tremor in her voice. "One that heals and one that kills. You can bring people back to life."

Lady Thanatou said nothing, and Helia felt she was speaking to a wall.

"I must repeat Teegan's question," she said. "Why did you choose to give Dolly death?"

"Have you ever stolen someone from their natural death?" Adara said. "Did you weigh the cost?"

Helia felt the question like a blow. Her face flushed, and

she thought of Art. "My . . . I understand. But again, the question remains: why do you bestow death?"

"Our lady does not execute," Adara answered coldly. "She grants what is asked."

"Did Rose Batts also choose suicide?" Helia said. It was easier to address Adara than face Lady Thanatou's piercing glare. "She, who could not envision herself beyond her humiliations and the outrages to her body . . . or perhaps it would not have suited your purpose to help her do so?"

Adara looked upon her, her gaze chilling. "You imply again that we favour death?"

"You have been called a 'death cult,'" Helia countered.

"The countess was syphilitic," Adara answered. "And Rose, made ill, desired her death to contribute to justice."

Helia took a deep breath. She could not fault Rose her decision. "And the woman on the bridge?" she said.

"That one, our lady intended to save," Adara said. "She was one who, when revived, might reconsider her intentions."

"Yet the sergeant interrupted," Helia said. "Was she restored?"

"Yes . . . she still chose to leap to her death. She was a poor woman, her children and husband lost to typhus. She too was ill, but our lady believed she would recover."

"Because hers was a body strong enough to survive the disease. Only her spirit could not," Helia said soberly. *I've nothing,* she thought. *There is no* pharmakos *ritual here.*

She then became aware that Adara had fallen silent and that Lady Thanatou stood nearer, still staring at Helia as if she were a bug meant to be squashed. "Why are you here?" she asked in a soft voice.

"I'm here to inquire as to your intentions, Lady Thanatou. You have been courting a young woman residing at the

Institute of the Blind, or should I say, seducing that young woman. And—"

Lady Thanatou's chin rose, and Helia saw her monocled eye flash. Helia's heart thundered. Dread filled her stomach and panic bloomed in her chest. She could not tear her gaze from Lady Thanatou's stare.

It's terror! I'm terrified! Helia thought.

Her knees gave way. She landed on the ground and her trembling left hand fluttered up to her mask. Lady Thanatou touched her own.

"No-no-no, don't!" Helia hissed to herself and grabbed her own left hand.

"'Ere now," Ellie exclaimed behind her. "Did you slip and fall, Helia? Should have known you'd tippled at luncheon." Ellie pulled her to her feet. "Set yourself on this bench now."

Ellie dragged her to the garden bench in question. With Ellie's body between her and Lady Thanatou, Helia could no longer look upon that baleful eye. Yet inexplicable fear still shook her, and Helia wrapped arms around herself. Adara, she noticed, had stepped away from her mistress, as if she too felt the effects of the eye.

"I must apologise for my friend. She 'as her weaknesses," Ellie said cheerfully to Lady Thanatou. "I'm Miss Hench. How d'ye do."

Helia heard no response. She dared to glance at Ellie, who stood, as she sometimes did in conversation, facing away from Lady Thanatou, as if there were an invisible person next to the woman. Ellie continued to converse to the empty space.

"Now, Miss Thanatou, as my drunk associate was sayin'. I've a very good friend, and it appears she's found a persistent admirer, that person being you. And even she suspects yer not a very ordinary suitor. But ordinary or not, what matters is whether you've good intentions."

Lady Thanatou took a deep breath and Helia turned away. A new wave of terror washed over her.

"This is what I think," Ellie continued. "You 'aven't killed anyone without them wanting it so, them ruffians bein' an unfortunate circumstance. As long as no one else dies, it would seem yer a respectable lady. Strange yet respectable, but London is filled with such strange ones, isn't it?" She stepped closer to Lady Thanatou, her voice measured. "I only hope to not see Elvie hurt."

"I do not wish her harmed, either," Lady Thanatou answered.

Ellie stood by Lady Thanatou, and Helia thought minutes passed with neither speaking another word. Not once did Ellie falter in Lady Thanatou's presence; her chin remained raised, her body at ease, and her odd grin was constant upon her lips. She finally cocked her head in Lady Thanatou's direction and spoke to the air above her shoulder.

"Thank you for the tea," she said and sauntered towards Helia, who stood shakily and took Ellie's arm. They walked into the house and Adara followed.

"My stick, if you please," Ellie called to no one in particular, and Adara hurried before them to disappear down the hall.

When they stepped out of the house and into the driveway, Helia let out a shaky gasp.

"You had quite the conversation with that 'ousekeeper; it was an 'elpful earful. But you failed miserably with 'er ladyship, Helia. 'Er magical eye got the best of you, I take it?" Ellie said, turning for their approaching carriage.

"*Its horror and its beauty are divine,*" Helia ejected. "Oh,

Ellie, that gaze! She purposefully worked it upon me." Helia felt once more that her knees might collapse. They boarded, and she sank in gratitude against the seat. As the carriage pulled away from the house, the dread in her stomach finally lessened. "You're fortunate that you are not affected."

"Oh, I felt the effects. But it took some time," Ellie said. "It was a chill that grew and grew. I've no idea how she did it, but if that's 'fascination,' then it'll be the first time I ever was entranced. Had I not bid good day when I did, I'd have been cryin' and wettin' myself, just like you."

"I assure you I did not wet myself."

"I'll begrudge you the assertion that I can be paralysed," Ellie said, her tone thoughtful. "Same as those ruffians. 'Ow she brought that Teegan back to the livin' was quite the feat."

"The restorative in the syringe must be her own blood," Helia said. "Taken from her right side, the healing side. Truly, she is the *pharmakon*."

"Certainly. Very farma-con. But as to 'er eye, Helia. Like you observed, it was an effect that needed to be worked, for I did not feel such in the museum. Nor did she ever try such a trick on Elvie, as far as I know. Elvie was only disturbed by that woman's forwardness, and 'erself being shy at the time. It had nothing to do with magical eyes."

"Yet," Helia said, "to have one like Lady Thanatou as suitor—"

"For one thing, there's somethin' not proper about you, Helia, yet Art's never been warned off from your taint."

Helia closed her eyes. "You are correct, Ellie."

"'Medusa the Queen,' you had said."

"I did."

"Well, she doesn't see Elvie as beneath 'er, and for now, Elvie finds this queen makes 'er 'appy. And she deserves all the 'appiness she can get. With Elvie in no danger of bein' dead sooner than she ought to be, upon this lady's word, which, if I agree with you, is a goddess's word, then I see no more reason to worry."

Helia nodded. "I agree, Ellie. There is nothing more we need do."

Chapter eleven

Ellie spent the rest of the evening accompanying Helia at Art's wrestling match and viewing Atlas's hirsute body and taut buttocks. She dined with the Skycourt twins at the Blue Vanda, then accompanied Helene back to Whitechapel where they parted. Ellie then visited her favourite dance hall and met a nimble-footed docker with a healthy, clean glow and strong hands. To his favour, he had a hairy chest. Ellie did not return to the Institute until very late and when all were in their beds sleeping.

Therefore, she did not visit Elvie until late the next morning, and found the young woman singing and rearranging her clays upon her shelves. Through Elvie's open door, the fluid world gave back to Ellie the taint between Elvie's eyes, which had grown.

Ellie shook her coin purse, gaining Elvie's attention, and entered her room.

"Elvie, me pocket's a jinglin'. 'Ow about joinin' me in a treat: a lark-and-kidney pudding at the Peacock. And as it will be near Bloomsbury, we may even dally at the museum."

"The Peacock? The Ophthalmic Hospital is by it, Ellie, on Grays Inn Road," Elvie said.

"Why, so it is."

"My uncle takes luncheon at the Peacock. As do many of his fellow surgeons. I fear our lark would be diminished should he spy us there."

"Why—"

"No, Ellie, I've plans for today. I don't want a meeting with my uncle to spoil it."

"You've been warblin' like a lark all mornin'. 'N I know the cause. Elvie, I shall be forthright. I witnessed yer departure from Lady Thanatou's 'ome yesterday, for I was just arrivin' to speak to 'er."

"You!" Elvie's hands turned to fists at her sides. "Oh, Ellie! What did you say to her? Oh! How dare you meddle!"

"Elvie, now you listen," Ellie said, her tone stern. "You know at the museum I witnessed 'er first, before she enticed you with 'er marbles 'n artist airs. And you know what I witnessed was an elephant. Can you fault me for making certain she weren't a danger to you—or to others?"

Elvie's chest heaved, but her life-glow no longer flared. "Well," she said, her tone stiff. "Is she?"

"For the moment, we've a civil disposition to the other, and that's a hard-won agreement, comin' from one like me."

Elvie relaxed more. "That is true, Ellie. You can be most difficult. Especially to those outside your circle. Have you been investigating her all this time?"

"I may 'ave. People 'ave been turnin' up all of stone since yer meetin' yer sculptress friend."

Elvie frowned. "I thought that was a cruel jest that awful custodian played on me. And the girl on the bridge? Was that not Sgt Trilby imagining things?"

"The matter's become more complex than that, though for you . . . perhaps it is no matter. Now." Ellie gentled her tone. "Would you like to ask me anythin' yer curious about, regardin' yer lady? I only offer should you truly want it."

"No. No, I believe I haven't questions. For she is coming to visit today, Ellie, and I—I'm enjoying the discoveries we share."

"That's good to 'ear, Elvie. Good indeed."

Mrs Darby fussed when Elvie informed her of the sculptress's impending visit, exclaiming on how the drawing room was hardly ready to receive a lady, nor did her kitchen have proper biscuits to serve. Finally she made the usual noises of resistance to a particular request.

"We've rules, Elvie," she said. "No visitors upstairs."

"But my clays are in my room and I want them viewed," Elvie argued. "Especially by an artist of her stature. Allow her to come upstairs, Mrs Darby, and I'll add a few more coins to the household fund."

Mrs Darby acquiesced after that, of course.

Elvie returned to her room, tidied it, though it needed no more cleaning, arranged her hair again, and then set her spectacles aside, deciding not to wear them. She sat and knitted. When she thought she heard the hum of an electric vehicle approach, she got up and hastily put her knitting away, touched her hair, then sat again. It wouldn't do to hurry downstairs, as much as she wanted to, but to be ladylike and await Mrs Darby.

She clasped and reclasped her hands, then discerned a commotion below. Frowning, she was wondering what the fuss might be when roses, pungent and strong, invaded her olfactory sense.

"*Hypíaine*, Elvie," the sculptress said.

Elvie's heart leapt to her throat and she stood up. "We do have a drawing room," she said, trying to slow her frantic heartbeat. "In which to properly meet."

"But you and your clays were not below," the sculptress said. "So I came to you." Elvie heard her door shut and footsteps fade in the hallway and realised that someone— Corrina, perhaps—had followed Lady Thanatou upstairs and then left.

"You certainly like to hasten matters," Elvie said. Had the lady remained silent upon entering her room and perhaps not smelled of roses, Elvie nonetheless doubted she would have missed her presence right then. She radiated heat; a sun's energy. She seemed to fill the room with tangibility.

"And what of tea?" Elvie said.

"Corrina may have it brought here."

"And what of your chaperone?"

Her answer was silence, though Elvie was certain the sculptress held her breath.

"Perhaps Mrs Darby would do?" Elvie offered politely.

"Yes," the sculptress said. "Yes, that one would do."

Elvie smiled. She held out her hand and the lady took it. "Please step this way to my very humble workspace," she said.

It was a single step, for her room, though larger than those for the other boarders, was hardly a fifth of the size of Lady Thanatou's studio. She possessed only a simple pedestal on which she modelled her clay (the present one being her fifth *Aphrodite*), and her shelves beside it, which displayed finished works. Before she could introduce her pieces, the lady gave a brief "ah!", stepped away, and began to inspect her shelves—at least Elvie assumed such by the movements the sculptress's body made. While Lady Thanatou perused, Elvie waited, a little impatient, and not a little anxious. She was about to say something when the sculptress finally spoke.

"*Kala*, Elvie. You are very good."

"I—what?"

"The eighth piece, it is the Asian water buffalo?"

"No, no, it is an elephant."

"Ahh. Beautiful, intriguing, and a powerful creature. I speak of your piece and am not discussing the true elephant. It is not necessary to know that you think your piece an elephant. To the sighted, it is a mysterious creature, great and noble. You have captured the virtues of the elephant and rendered them here."

"I did? Well, yes, mysterious," Elvie said. "The elephant does have its secrets. I am very good?"

"You," the sculptress said, her voice low and suddenly very close. "Are a lover of form."

Elvie took a step back. "I am, but you are a master of it."

"Mine is learning, nothing more. Yours is *kardia*. You have the heart, the seat of feeling, such learning needs."

Is that what you need? Elvie thought. *Is that what you are seeking, in copying hurt figures?* Overwhelmed by the thought, she had no response, and a silence ensued.

"Elvie, I must ask," Lady Thanatou then said lightly. "The fifth clay upon your shelf?"

Elvie put a hand to her mouth and giggled. "It is my attempt at a *fascinum*."

"And why would you attempt so, Elvie? I see three here. Have you need of . . . protection?"

"Oh no." Elvie smiled. "I became aware of a special

collection locked away inside the British Museum —"

"The erotic collection," the lady said in a dry tone.

"Oh yes. I'm no longer allowed back there, either. Well, the subject is intriguing, that the vulgar phallus — and its female equivalent — were used in ancient times as charms to draw the attention of the Evil Eye. Or any such ill attentions. I could not grasp the idea, perhaps because I don't possess eyes, but after modelling a winged phallus, I think I may understand the nature of its fascination. For the sighted always notice it, this penis. I even made an anthropomorphic one. It has literally caught an eye in its arms. Do you like the jest?"

"I do."

Elvie smiled, then sighed. "However, such protective charms are not well received in our society, so I've been discouraged from making tiny ones as Christmas presents. It's not a terribly accurate facsimile of the male sexual organ, is it?"

"For Dionysus's orgiastic cults, it would be favourable," the lady said.

Elvie giggled again. She sensed the sculptress turning away, perhaps to view her clays more.

"But your fashioning of the female pudendum is a most realistic facsimile, Elvie."

"Well I — well, yes," Elvie said.

She detected a slight sound from her shelves, as if the sculptress had picked up the clay.

"It draws my eye," Lady Thanatou said softly.

Someone knocked at her door. "Come in?" Elvie said faintly, uncertain if she wanted that someone to enter. Mrs Darby shuffled heavily as she opened the door.

"Pardon me, your ladyship," Mrs Darby said. "I just

wanted to ask if Elvie would like tea served here."

"Oh yes, Mrs Darby. Thank you," Elvie said, suspecting Mrs Darby was more likely looking in to see if all was well. Corrina murmured in the hallway as she and Mrs Darby discussed the serving of tea, and the door shut again.

"What are you wearing today?" Elvie said. She thought she might have startled Lady Thanatou again. Her question was met with silence. "I ask because I understand that the sighted's strongest visual impression of a person might be in the colour they wear. I want to know if today your dress is different from what you wore when we first became aware of each other. At the museum."

She heard the lady hum, and the sound neared, accompanied by the hint of fabric rustling. Elvie thought that if she listened for that and not for footfalls, then she might know the sculptress's movements.

You gave me your footstep's sound at the museum, and at the party, and when I returned to your home, Elvie thought. *But now . . . .*

She sensed the sculptress's heat before her.

"At the museum," the sculptress said, her tone thoughtful. "I wore 'night.'"

"Oh? Like the deepest time?"

"Of slumber, yes. It is what I wear every day."

"But today?" Elvie said, smiling.

"Today, I wear . . . apple."

"The sour sort?"

"Oh no. The sweetest sort, Elvie."

"Ah. I understand that to be a beautiful colour. Would your dress be the perfection of Eve's apple?"

The lady laughed, but it was with her lips or teeth closed, the sound remaining in her throat. Elvie wanted to put her fingers on that throat and feel the vibration.

"Perhaps," the sculptress said, her tone warm.

"Thank you for not giving me the names of colours. You have a . . . an intimate understanding of the blind," Elvie said. "Especially we who were never sighted."

"Many of my companions have been so."

Elvie breathed from the thrill such admittance gave her. She felt flushed. "Why is that? That you should keep the company of the blind?"

"Mine is a countenance that should never be witnessed."

Elvie frowned in dismay. "Have you . . . injury?"

"None that hurts presently. But my face is a complicated matter."

Elvie raised her hands.

Lady Thanatou's own hands guided them to her face. Elvie felt the metal mask again, brushing across for the nose and finding it obscured, though the high contour of the mask told her the sculptress might possess a straight nose. She moved her touch carefully up, encountering no eyeholes, either; she felt nothing but smoothness across the left side of the face, and met a protruding lense on the right, similar to the one on Sgt Trilby's camera. She tried to avoid the glass and in running her finger along the rim, discovered a tiny protrusion: a button. She accidentally compressed it.

Click.

Elvie stilled, surprised. The sound was distinctly that of a camera's shutter. Before she could ask, the lady laughed, the mirth once more held within her throat. Elvie ran her hands down to feel the vibration, and the sculptress raised her chin to comply. She felt the last sound of laughter against her fingertips and something else just beneath the dress collar. Elvie touched along the line of a thin, clean scar.

In wonder, she followed the scar from the sculptress's throat to her nape, pushing her fingers beneath the weight of the heavy snood, weighted by more than hair. Elvie caressed the heaviness, feeling . . . ropey, long . . . hot . . . .

The sculptress grasped both her wandering hands in one of hers, then took hold of Elvie's chin. She felt the sudden press of lips on hers.

Oh, mouth, Elvie thought. The sculptress's lips were soft and full, sending her trembling. Elvie pressed back and one of her hands escaped. She touched the sculptress's face again as they kissed, brushing across once more. She bumped against the heavy snood, and it undulated.

Elvie froze beneath the sculptress's mouth. The snood rustled, and something coiled around her fingers. Something else seized her fingertip—small, a mouth. A tiny mouth that didn't let go.

A scream rose within Elvie. Before the sound released, the tiny mouth vanished. Her finger was freed, and the lady's lips left hers. Elvie staggered.

Where the sculptress once stood, Elvie felt only air. She reached with her hands, her hearing; inhaled, and smelled her nowhere. Her door bumped against the wall and Elvie started.

The sound in her throat escaped, a strangled cry. She clutched the afflicted finger and found no holes, no blood seeping, yet her body would not obey her brain's assertion. Her head went light. She swayed and thought of asps and poisons.

When she fell to her knees, she barely heard the smooth hum of the electric vehicle below, speeding away.

A year ago, a new freak show opened in Whitechapel, and Elvie gave a coin to the snake lady for the privilege of touching a snake. The snake was muscular, textured, and surprisingly warm. She listened to the flicking of its tongue. Then the snake lady agitated one of her pets so Elvie could hear how a threatened snake sounded. The rasping hiss, repeated, became a frightening noise. The woman explained how the snake moved, wrapped its body around prey, and struck with its fangs. Elvie placed her hands on the snake lady's arm to feel her imitate the motion of striking.

Snakes. Hair. The custodian. Elvie sat in her room and put a fist to her pained forehead. She reviewed everything, every detail she knew about her sculptress, and the remarks Ellie had casually given.

"People of stone," she whispered.

Mrs Darby had wondered at Lady Thanatou's abrupt departure and seeing Elvie upset, assumed the appreciation of her clays had not gone well. Elvie shut her door on her fellow boarders to dissuade discussion or sympathies. She took dinner in her room, ate little, ingested headache powders for her poor head, and paced her room. Her mind could not still.

She left her room to search for Ellie, only to learn that her friend was still out escorting. Elvie resigned herself to bed, but once asleep she dreamt of nothing but sibilant sounds, of small mouths biting her. Then she dreamt of herself made of marble, frozen and mute, while strange hands touched her.

Elvie woke, sweating and still possessed of terror.

When morning came, she eschewed breakfast, still not willing to discuss the sculptress's visit, and sat at her table, slowly folding writing paper. Her copy of Thomas

Bulfinch's *The Age of Fable, or Stories of Gods and Heroes* lay aside, having been shut repeatedly and violently on the entry regarding the Gorgon, only for Elvie to flip through and consult it again, as if hoping the braille had changed. Memory of the neck scar she'd touched, the hisses she'd heard, came to the fore.

"'I keep snakes,'" she recalled and laughed harshly.

The conclusion, after a night and morning of heart's upheaval, was undeniable. Elvie decided to accept it and ignore her tumultuous state, recollect her thoughts and her composure. Folding paper was like brushing stone; its sounds soothed and thrilled, and she needed the calm such activity brought. She listened to the stiff paper rustle as she smoothed the folds. Each long crease gave a soft *brooosh* beneath her fingers, and every turn of the paper emitted a crinkle. She fabricated paper spoons, cups, birds, and boats. A pile of paper toys grew before her. Yet a deep, sick feeling resided in her heart that no soothing aural sensation could still.

"Monster? What is that?" she said. "And killer? Yes, killer. Would you argue against her nature?"

She recalled the custodian's last breath, issued on the surface of her fingertips. Elvie shuddered and dropped the folded paper.

Ellie whistled a sea shanty tune in the hall, and Elvie stood.

"Ellie!" she called. *"Ellie!"*

"Ho-ho, Elvie, what's the matter?" Ellie said at her open door. "What fire?"

"Did you know?" Elvie asked, her tone accusing. "Did you know what she was? How could you not tell me, when she has viperine hair—all of snakes!"

"I—" Ellie said. "Snakes . . . y'mean to say, *true* snakes, Elvie? Lady Thanatou? Why . . . that certainly makes 'er tale even more 'orrific."

"Ellie, believe me, her locks are of snakes. Alive, hissing, and deadly."

"Alive? 'N 'ere I thought Helia meant very awful hair, which made the beheadin' story seem a bit much. I thought it all a frizzle like the hair of freak-show women, pouffed—"

"Ellie, how could you not know!"

"She wears a snood of *solid* cloth, Elvie. I couldn't know wot's beneath it, like a nun and 'er wimple."

Elvie sat again and held her head. She heard Ellie step close.

"She was the one who made the custodian stone," Elvie said, her voice strained. "Yet brought him back again. And also the woman on the bridge."

"'N a few others, Elvie."

"Oh Ellie, the girl," Elvie said in realisation. "*The Slave.*"

"Aye, that, though that's a complicated matter. Just know that some *wanted* to be made stone, Elvie."

"But why?" Elvie cried.

"For suicide, Elvie, she makes it easier for them. To end an illness, especially. Though her ladyship has been accused of makin' it a religious affair—'death cult' was the accusation. I'm still ponderin' that."

Elvie pressed both her palms against her forehead, and Ellie laid a comforting hand on her shoulder. "'Er hair. Is it as bad as that, Elvie?"

"It isn't—" she said.

"If I met a man with two or three spouters, I might run off screamin'. Yes, I do believe I would." She patted Elvie in reassurance. "It's for the best, then."

"I'm acting like a sighted person. It's not just—" When she spoke no further, Ellie patted her once more. Elvie thought of Thana and suppressed the sudden thought that she didn't want to voice: *But does she want to make a statue of me?*

"I must think," she whispered.

"Ellie," Mrs Darby called from the hallway.

"I'm in 'ere, Mrs Darby," Ellie answered.

"Your, ah, that acquaintance," Mrs Darby said at the door. "She insists on coming—I—oh! Well!" Her exclamations faded, and a brief discussion ensued in the hall. Elvie heard the high-heeled steps of a woman as she entered her room.

"Hello, hello!" the woman said gaily. "I apologise for the intrusion. You must be Miss Elvie Chaisty?"

"I am," Elvie said, perplexed. She felt a card pressed into her hand, and she ran her fingers over the embossed lettering.

"I am Miss Helia Skycourt, journalist for the *Times*. How do you do. But I'm not here in that capacity, Miss Chaisty."

Elvie explored the card again, loving the feel of the paper. "How do you do." She held out her hand in a vague direction and Helia's gloved one grasped it firmly. "Ellie has spoken of you, Miss Skycourt."

"Then I hope she also told you of the legendary wrestling match two of His Royal Highness's Secret Commission agents have been engaged in, over at Chelsea. I wanted Ellie to know posthaste that Art won."

"Wot news, Helia! Three days and nights they been at it. 'Ow did she take 'im?"

"Not by splitting his trousers again, much to your and many a woman's disappointment. In their final stages of fatigue, she merely lifted him, and as he suffers from the same weakness as his mythical namesake, he conceded.

Your winnings, Miss Hench." A purse of coins jingled.

"Oh, what a fine weight," Ellie said, admiration in her tone. "Thank you, Helia. I'm certain the poor fellow will be needin' comfortin' after such a defeat."

Helia giggled. "Is that longing I hear, Ellie? He should have taken the namesake Heracles. He is buried beneath his many women at the moment."

"Humph. Harem," Ellie sniffed.

"Or are they more his trophies? As would suit a superior being?" Elvie remarked, and she surprised herself by her own sharp tone. She blushed as a silence fell upon the room.

"Erm," Ellie said. "M'Lady Monocle called upon Elvie, Helia. I'm afraid it did not go well."

"Oh, Miss Chaisty!"

"Please." The sympathy embarrassed her. "I'm simply trying to get used to the—well, my learning of her true nature."

"Ah, yes. That can be surprising knowledge, Miss Chaisty. And you believe Lady Thanatou collects . . . trophies?"

Elvie realised her error, voicing assumptions that might compromise the sculptress before a journalist. But the question nagged at her. She thought again of Thana, of how beautiful she'd felt her features to be, how noble her bearing. How her breasts, belly, and hips were more womanly than her own.

Is that also why I'm afraid—angry? she thought. "Miss Skycourt, would you know what a *hetaera* is?" she asked instead.

"Ah, your question recalls my studies of Pericles's Athens. Why yes, Miss Chaisty. A *hetaera* is an independent, educated, and very sophisticated woman of Greece whose role was as a valued companion. A courtesan, if you will."

"A prostitute, you mean," Elvie said.

"That is sometimes the meaning, Miss Chaisty, though their class is considered higher and distinguished from such."

"Such women must abound in Greece, I suppose."

"Do you mean presently? Oh no, such interesting women are as obsolete as their Greek gods. We are speaking of a time more than two thousand years past."

"Two thousand years!"

"Miss Chaisty?" Helia said.

"It is one thing to know someone and think them different, Miss Skycourt. It is quite another for that someone to now be—"

"A monster?" Ellie said.

"A goddess?" Helia said.

"It is neither of those," Elvie said wearily. She wiped at her eyes sockets. "I—now I can't help recalling our times together with different intentions. But what does 'truth' matter, really? Her truth. My truth. In the end, I am still fascinated by her."

"That doesn't 'ave to be an 'elpless feeling." Elvie heard Ellie shift her feet. "In such a case, you take on matters and ask 'er to go dancin'."

Elvie felt a touch on her arm; from the direction of the touch, she thought it from Miss Skycourt.

"You should take the time to accept this latest revelation, Miss Chaisty," she said, her tone sympathetic. "Then, as Ellie has said, pursue when you are ready."

Elvie heard the tinkle of a watch chain from Ellie's direction.

"We must depart, Elvie. I have to escort Helia to Billingsgate. But you take 'eart now."

"Yes, Ellie." She straightened. "I do feel better, truly."

They both moved for her door, and she did her best to keep her bearing stronger than she felt. She nearly dropped the posture when she heard Helia speak in parting.

"And I hope you'll remember, Miss Chaisty. You in turn fascinate her."

Chapter Twelve

Elvie spent the next two days immersed in teaching, knitting stockings, scratching long marks into writing paper with steel-tipped dip pens, and folding them into piles of boats until she ran out of paper. She barely touched her clays. At dinnertime, when Mrs Darby and the other boarders gossiped about strange, foreign men loitering near the Institute, she paid the discussion no mind. She thought of nothing but the sculptress, and when Ellie tried to coax her into a trip to the Peacock and Bloomsbury again, Elvie dismissed her outright, feeling she would no longer find comfort in Room 84. However, she did agree to take a stroll with Ellie, for her temper had been short and her fellow boarders' tolerance was coming to an end. When she descended, hat and stick in hand, she heard Mrs Darby.

"After these last two stone people were discovered, well! Trilby would bend any ear that would listen, regarding his own statue story. Even boasted to me that a foreign man interviewed him for some foreign paper."

"What sort of foreign man?" Ellie asked.

Elvie stepped upon the landing and heard a faint "halloo!" from a man outside.

"Oh! The coal's arrived. If you'll excuse me, Ellie."

Elvie tapped her way to where she thought Ellie might be while Mrs Darby's heavy steps faded away.

"Well, Elvie, yer rejection might 'ave been upsettin' for 'er 'ighness," Ellie said when Elvie reached her side. "The papers say two more women 'ave been found, turned to stone."

"What?" Elvie uttered.

"Gist of the matter is, they sound like suicides. Perhaps better that than them joining the offal floatin' beneath Blackfriars Bridge."

"This is terrible," Elvie whispered.

"No need to worry, Elvie, Helia has her sweetheart involved presently, to resolve the matter. Elephant to elephant, you might say."

"What do you mean? Who is Miss Skycourt's sweetheart?" Elvie said, her stomach dropping.

"Why, Artifice, of course, who recently defeated Atlas."

Elvie grabbed for Ellie, missed, then tried again. She contacted Ellie's arm. "We must stop her!" she said. She gripped Ellie tightly.

"Elvie," Ellie said. "I'm certain they'll only 'ave words. Unless 'er goddesship turns Helia to stone. Even a Quaker should take offence at that."

"That's why we must go, Ellie! To Lady Thanatou's house. I no longer care about the danger to myself."

"Wot danger to you?" Ellie said, her tone startled.

"Which way is the front door? I'm all turned around."

"Elvie, wot danger?"

"Of my being—oh Ellie! Added to her marble collection!"

"Bosh, Elvie, she assured me she wouldn't, goddess's word. Put on yer hat—there's a girl. 'Ere's the door."

"Truly? And you thought to tell me this when?" Elvie cried.

"Well, I—I thought you didn't like 'er hair, Elvie," Ellie said. "'Er nature, and such. A matter irreconcilable, it seemed. And did it not occur to you that without yer eyeballs, perhaps you mightn't become a marble?"

Elvie stopped on the walk, mouth dropping, then blushed. She pulled on Ellie again.

"No matter. I was troubling myself like a foolish sighted person. We must hurry!"

"Certainly. But you've gone alone twice, Elvie," Ellie said with suspicion. "Why must I go with you now?"

"Because you've fought the agent before, Ellie. And I will give you ten guineas to do it again."

⁓

They rode a swift hansom cab to South Kensington and Brompton, Ellie noting that a cab would travel faster than the hackney carriage. Like the open-air phaeton, an open-air cab was a rare ride, but the wind and sun on Elvie's face could no more reassure her than her attempts to soothe her nerves with the sounds of folding paper and pen scratches.

"Elvie, you really thought she could turn you to stone?" Ellie asked.

"I'm a bit ashamed at the fear I gave myself. But . . . I'd never felt sightless with her, Ellie. And she never seemed like one of the sighted to me—you know how I mean. The way they dismiss us, or patronise us. How they don't understand us, our world. I felt she always knew me and I, her, and perhaps it was that intimacy that convinced me,

most irrationally, that I could fall under any enchantment
she could work on me."

"It's a most potent gaze she has," Ellie said. "Even I 'ave
felt it. I've a widow's veil ruinin' the pretty brim of me hat
for that reason. It's meant to obscure my own perceptions.
But I'm still able to 'look' at 'er, Elvie. In my peculiar way.
You can't."

"No, Ellie, I believe I can. I just explained it to you." She
twined her fingers in her lap, fretting. "But perhaps now I've
ruined everything."

Ellie patted her hand. "Silly Elvie. Never consider
anythin' done forever."

Elvie wanted to agree, but her affirmation stuck in her
throat. If she couldn't make amends with the sculptress or
prevent her being harmed by Artifice, Elvie felt her heart
would be destroyed. Ellie sat back, crunching the leather of
their seat while Elvie perched tensely beside her.

"Last I was there, they served me tea in tiny glasses," Ellie
remarked. "With sticky cakes adrip with 'oney. And they'd
walnuts in 'em. The sweets were as jewelled as 'er Majesty's
crown. They told me the treats were Turkish."

"Then you'll be content to remain in their drawing room
and give no fuss?"

"I thought you wanted me to fight Art."

"I only want—oh! This Artifice must listen to me! I want
nothing to happen. Nothing."

"I'm content with 'nothing.' As long as they feed me those
queer cakes and biscuits, I'll be a queen made all over with
spun sugar lacin'."

Helia sat in a hansom cab with Art and watched Kensington's shops and homes give way to more bucolic surroundings. The air freshened and birds sang. Though she was hardly a proper lady, she still favoured closed carriages, as was *de rigueur* for respectable women, but Art loved the open cabs. Art looked about in interest, exclaimed on the pretty scenery with its hidden cottages and manors, market gardens and nurseries, and grasped Helia's hand.

"I've spied a tavern, Helia, the Hoop and Toy. Dost thee think it may have a fish for me and a pie for thee?"

"I believe it would, dearest," Helia said warmly, ignoring their surroundings to gaze up at Art.

When their cab entered the avenue leading to Thanatou's home, Art asked if they were in a hurry, and Helia said they were not. Art then requested the cab stop for them to alight and ride ahead to their destination. Standing upon the tree-canopied avenue, she set her ironwood walking stick to the ground and offered her arm.

"Walk with me, dear Helia," she said, and Helia accepted happily.

Female cyclists approached and sped past in single file, but Helia paid them no mind. In full sunlight, Art's eldritch glow was not as apparent, and her ghostly paleness could be mistaken for albinism. She was solid, warm, and smelled of violets, and Helia hugged Art's arm to her.

"Thee and Manon seemed civil these past few days," Art said as they strolled.

"I want us very much to be civil," Helia said. "I may have a mal—mal—maledic—dichotomy! But Manon knows how to soothe matters."

She felt Art pat her hand, and when she looked up at her kind face, Helia realised her eldritch infection had stolen her words again.

"I have thee, Manon, and Helene in my heart," Art said. "Yet Atlas keeps six women. Six! And he with one penis."

Helia's laughter startled birds within the canopy, and leaves fluttered down.

"Jim says Friend Thunder is also spouse to some of the women. Their heart-family is queerly polyaphroditic! But I am happy for them and wish them prosperity should they have eighteen offspring."

The last was wryly said, and Helia glanced up at Art with keen interest. "Are you curious, dear, as to the amorous habits of the one we are visiting?" she asked.

Art squeezed her hand in affirmation. "I know we creatures, created by Dr Fall and the Secret Commission, are written into living by alchemic formula," she said. "We are new beings, and I am but three months living. The one we are meeting is so very old, come to the world in the conventional manner: of woman. In matters of the heart, her pantheon seems also to love conventionally. Perhaps we new beings, borne in science and lightning, can't help our modern aspect."

"It is my hope that you may never suffer our human failings," Helia said, "but transcend them."

"How great thy wishes are," Art said, her tone soft. "No transcendence need happen if thee is not there in the joining." She lifted Helia's hand and kissed it.

Helia's heart swelled, fit to burst.

Art looked down at her and smiled. "Now I wonder," she said. "How shall I speak to one older than e'en Manon, who can recall Charlemagne?"

"You must present your most imposing figure to Lady Thanatou, dear Art."

"Thee requires that I intimidate," Art said, her protestation mild.

"Dearest, she is a being hard to impress. She thinks myself an infected bug and Ellie, well, a mere thug. But you; you are certain to earn her attention."

"She is one sired by sea gods," Art mused. "Manon thought that a powerful thing."

"You could be a godling, Art," Helia said.

Art halted their walk and touched Helia's hand. "Oh, thee not say such a thing," she exclaimed. "Oh, to e'en think! 'Twould be so very above my Light. Thee speaks in jest. Assure me."

"I speak with adoration and love," Helia said. "I worship you."

She picked up Art's gloved hand and kissed it in return. As they strolled beneath the shade and spotlights of sun shining through the tree-canopied avenue, she wished they could walk on and forget about Lady Thanatou and her statues. She paused before a driveway hidden from view by a thick hedge.

"Here is the house." She took a deep breath, searched in her dress pocket, then presented Art with her hand mirror. "And here is your defence, should you need it."

———

Adara stood within the portico with Ahmet, watching their approach, and Helia thought her manner and gaze surprisingly genial. She bowed to Art and gave her a formal welcome, and Art answered with a kind greeting. As Helia expected, Adara ignored her, making her feel more like the pet monkey hanging on Art's arm.

With their reception more or less civil, Helia's nervousness was somewhat placated. Adara took Art's ironwood and led them down the vestibulum for the peristylium proper. She bade Art tour the marbles at leisure until Lady Thanatou could receive them, then offered refreshments. After Art asked if Helia required any, Art graciously declined, and Adara left them to enjoy the garden.

Art looked about. "Where is Rose Batts, Helia?" she asked.

Art's viewing of Rose's marble was somber, and once she was done she kissed the statue upon its forehead. She and Helia moved on to other pieces, ambling in comfortable companionship and stopping often to remark and admire. Helia did not spy any more marbles that seemed formerly human; the evidence was in the details, with the mark of a chisel upon hair, clothing, or the figure itself. Often the faces depicted classical ideals practiced through the centuries. If the figures had a sense of individuality, the size of them (often smaller than lifesize) resolved the suspicion. Helia felt that except for Rose Batts, the rest of the marbles appeared created by hand and not by a Gorgon's gaze.

Art approached each piece without apparent worry as to its origins and enjoyed many of the themes and remarkable executions, for Helia believed that Lady Thanatou's hand and eye were very talented indeed. Often, Art asked Helia to explain a myth depicted. She was still musing on the circumstance of Leda lying with Zeus in the form of a swan when they came upon a muscular male torso exerting great power in its straining frame.

"'Tis Atlas!" Art exclaimed to Helia's surprise. She pointed at his chest, as if even without his body hair she would know his impressive pectoral muscles. Helia decided to agree, though she herself could not make the identification, even when looking at his buttocks.

"Indeed, Art. And he requires a substantial fig leaf," Helia remarked. Her face suddenly itched, and she turned, seeing no one else in the peristylium but the waving ferns and the still, white marbles.

Art walked on with Helia and stopped to regard a sensual female torso, its garments pulled down to reveal its buttocks. If Art knew Lady Thanatou was present in the garden, she gave no sign. She studied the torso's front with keen interest while Helia looked furtively about. When she glanced up, Art was regarding something beyond the torso, her gaze curious. Art returned her attention to the torso once more, studied it, then looked up again, smiling. Helia took a step away from Art to peek around the piece.

There stood Lady Thanatou in black and purple, several paces away, her golden mask gleaming. Her body was sideways, her chin low, and Helia thought that if Thanatou wished to rush at them, even Art might be hard pressed to stop her. Adara stood in calm attendance behind her lady, and Lady Thanatou slowly raised her chin, her gold monocle flashing in the sunlight. Art moved forwards with Helia on her arm.

"How prospers truth in thy parts, Friend?" Art greeted. "Thine is a weighty torso."

The lady did not answer, though Helia thought her full, red lips almost curled into a smile. But the hint of such disappeared when the lady's blue eye suddenly dropped to regard Helia.

Helia felt her insides shrivel like a moth curling in a flame. She could not bear a third examination of her tainted soul and turned to hide behind Art.

"Helia?" Art said in concern.

"She sees me!" Helia said as she clung to Art's back. "Oh,

she sees me, Art!"

Art pressed her to her back.

"I love thee," Art said as she looked behind at Helia. "Stay with me, for I'll not have thee suffer alone."

Helia felt another wave of terror and said nothing. Art's back straightened beneath her clinging grip.

"Friend," Art said, her tone chastising. "Must thee torment?"

Then Helia heard Lady Thanatou deliberately step. She saw her circle around, the lady's gaze not on her but seemingly appraising Art instead, with a keen fascination. Helia scurried around while Lady Thanatou continued to walk, until Helia ended up behind Art again. She heard Lady Thanatou stop before Art.

"May our lady take your photograph, Artifice?" Adara politely asked.

Helia's eyes widened. Art acquiesced, and Helia heard a distinct click. She peeked and saw Lady Thanatou touching the side of her monocle. When she removed her finger, Helia spied the tiny button she'd compressed.

"Would you also consider posing for our lady?" Adara asked.

"Oh," Art said in surprise. She turned her head and looked at Helia behind her. "Would it not please Helene to have a nude figure of myself, Helia?"

Helia could only nod, thinking Helene might be more dumbstruck by such a gift than merely pleased.

Art turned back to Lady Thanatou. "'Twould be my pleasure. And, Friend," she said. "I thank thee for ceasing thy baleful gaze."

Adara took a breath to reply, but it was Lady Thanatou who spoke.

"Why do you keep such company?" she asked, her quiet tone curious.

"'Tis a love unexplainable," Art said. "As love is. I would have it no other way."

She reached behind her, and guided Helia to her side again. Helia blushed, feeling ridiculous, but Lady Thanatou ignored her, her single eye upon Art.

"I thank thee for this meeting, for I come bearing a concern, Friend," Art said. "A concern for those who have met their Light upon their own choosing."

Art paused and Lady Thanatou stared, but her gaze, Helia thought, seemed receptive.

"'Tis said that thee is a queen amongst women," Art continued. "But I believe in our commonality, Friend, e'en as uncanny ones, thee and me. I hope that thee may bear the substance of my thoughts with thy heart clear."

"What are your words?" Adara asked.

"Cease thy rescue of these women who utilise thee for suicide," Art said. "I question not thy judgement but theirs. And if they still intend to end life without thy help, then it shall be so. 'Tis not a task thee should bear. I believe thee knows this too."

"You should not be their cult of death," Helia quickly added.

Lady Thanatou's eye fixed upon her again, and the malevolent glare made Helia feel she might turn to ice and shatter.

⌖

Elvie felt their cab come to a stop, and while Ellie paid the driver, Ahmet opened the cab door and helped Elvie out.

"Miss, it is good to see you," he said. She heard the light footfall of a woman on the drive's gravel and hid her disappointment, knowing the steps did not belong to the sculptress.

"Miss," Corrina said. "Welcome. But how grave your expression! Is something the matter?"

"Please, Corrina," Elvie said. "I must speak to her."

"Yes, miss. Right away."

Elvie linked arms with Ellie and walked quickly. They paused within the vestibule for Corrina to take their sticks, then hurried on again.

"She is in the garden, miss, with Artifice, the Secret Commission agent, and—her companion," Corrina said.

"Corrina, I must interrupt them. And Ellie comes with me."

"Of course, miss."

"Weren't I to eat cakes, Elvie?" Ellie asked mildly as they hurried along.

"Not until we've stopped the elephants, Ellie," Elvie said. She heard wind chimes, and their feet reached the softness of earth and paving. The light breeze brought the beguiling scent of roses mixed with frankincense.

"Thee persists, Friend?" Elvie heard a woman say, and she thought the tone weighted.

"Our lady's patience with that one is at an end," Adara said, her voice cold.

"'Ello, 'ello. Elvie would like a word, if it pleases yer ladyship, 'n I believe it does. Artifice, this is Elvie, Elvie, Artifice. Would you and yer ladyship mind steppin' back as Elvie likes her room? Here you are, Elvie." And Ellie thrust Elvie against a tall woman's body—very tall—who exuded body heat to rival the sculptress's. The tall woman touched her back, steadying her. Elvie found Artifice's arms and gripped the tops of pronounced biceps.

Oh, what muscles! Elvie thought. *Oh my!*

"This is Miss Elvie Chaisty, Art," she heard Helia say as Elvie felt along Art's forearms. "She is the woman whom Lady Th—"

Helia ceased speaking, giving a strangled sound. Art's body seemed to grow harder beneath Elvie's palms, like strength coiling, and a chill raised the hairs on Elvie's neck.

"Stop that," she snapped to the air, and then regretted her tone. "I—please."

The chill ceased. But Art's body remained tense, and Elvie felt upwards in desperation. The agent seemed to go on forever.

"'When I consider how my light was spent,'" she said in urgency.

Art's body relaxed beneath her hands; it seemed she had her attention. But Elvie, overcome with passion, could not say more. She forgot the rest of the poem's words; she forgot what she meant to say.

"Helia?" Art queried.

Helia cleared her throat, somewhere behind Art. "It is a poem by Milton, dearest." Her voice quavered. "It is the lament of a blind person, questioning how he may serve his God. For being blind, he, or she, feels inadequate to the task . . . when compared with the sighted."

"That is not so," the sculptress ejected behind Elvie. Elvie's heart leapt, but she continued to cling to Art and felt her large, warm hands rise to her shoulders. The contact was meant to comfort, yet she did not know if such touch was to assure Elvie that her desire to keep the sculptress safe would be granted, or reassure her against an outcome undesirable.

Oh please! she thought. *Please do not harm each other!*

"This poem, Helia," Art said. "How doth it end?"

"'They also serve who stand and waite,' 'They' meaning those made blind, Art."

Art raised Elvie's hands, then bent down. Elvie touched soft lips that quirked at the corners. It was a mouth that smiled: warm, gentle, and generous.

"Is thee ready to serve thy heart-friend, Elvie?" Art said kindly.

Elvie could not speak; she tried to nod, as sighted were said to do, and bumped her forehead into Art's bosom instead. Art straightened, and when she spoke, it was over Elvie's head.

"Hast thee not this thought: 'how fortunate am I that I am loved'?" Art said. "Thee has a champion. One who laid down our near conflict with her words, heart to hand. Would thee agree, Friend?"

Elvie listened; she heard nothing more except the tinkle of wind chimes.

"And would thee agree as well, there will be no more suicides by thy aid?"

Again, Elvie heard nothing, and she was about to express her frustration when she was turned around and then led to another who reached for her. The sculptress's hands grasped hers and pulled her close.

"Joy is mine and thine, Friend," Art said.

***

Elvie stood close to a body's scent and warmth she knew, and giddiness suffused her. She heard Art and Helia step away, speaking in low voices to each other, and Ellie — wherever she might be, Elvie knew Ellie could take care of herself and might already be speculating about tea.

"Thank you," she said happily.

"For what, Elvie?" the lady said. Elvie squeezed the hands in hers. Her throat loosened and her body relaxed. She no longer felt overwhelmed by the presence of so startling an elephant as Art.

"Perhaps concession is not what a—a *great* being like yourself would consider. Therefore, thank you," Elvie said.

"It was a simple decision," the sculptress said.

"And I'm sorry for my sudden withdrawal," Elvie said. "That was rude and unkind. But I had felt that, already, you've a power over me. And now that I know you are — well, such a being. Then you could have me completely, couldn't you? Just eat up little Elvie. That notion simply frightened me."

Lady Thanatou laughed, the sound clear and womanly, and Elvie wanted to feel it in the movement of the lady's shoulders, of her chest, if she could hold her.

"The things you say, Elvie," the sculptress said, her tone warm.

"I'm sorry I became frightened," Elvie said. "I must learn, with you. And I should know better. People find my own lack of eyeballs quite a fright."

"No, you are perfect, Elvie. And when I first saw you at the museum . . . ." The sculptress moved close. "I thought you perfect for me."

Elvie shivered. She felt that familiar intoxication of both joy and trepidation, as when stepping into a wide, open space and not knowing where she stood in it. "I will be presumptuous and assume that something may occur between us, and it is something I welcome. But whatever the outcome, be it so very short or . . . not so short. And should my ability to amuse you draw to its swift end, I shall make a most bold request. Oh, you make me tremble so!"

The sculptress released her hands and touched her. "What is it, Elvie?"

"I simply need an assurance. I want to be returned safely to the Institute of the Blind. In good health! As I am now. Whenever—whenever you tire." She swallowed. "Won't you promise me?"

She listened. Though Lady Thanatou still touched her, the contact no longer seemed intimate. Elvie felt a distance suddenly created.

"What is it?" she asked. Her fear grew.

Then she heard a shout, as if from within the house. It was abrupt and cut short, and she thought it Ahmet's. The sculptress left her, and Elvie heard running feet, sounding not like a woman's but a man's heavy—

The air exploded before and behind her. Elvie felt the shattering bangs like blows to her head and clapped hands over her ears. Someone yelled and scents jumbled: burning powder, fresh blood, frankincense, male sweat. The sweating man grabbed her just as a sickening snap sounded in the air, like chicken bones breaking.

Elvie heard ragged breath, felt the man's rough grip, then something sharp—excruciating, *biting*—pierced her neck. Elvie screamed.

CHAPTER THIRTEEN

Ellie thought the peace made between the Quaker and the supposed goddess a tidy resolution, and with all parties seemingly content, hoped tea might be announced soon, or more appropriately, stronger stuff served to wet her whistle.

The sudden entry of four male shapes from four different directions gave Ellie two choices to protect, and she chose the nearest one, caught in the coming crossfire of two gun wielders. She grabbed Helia and dove to the ground, feeling bullets spiral through the fluid world and strike Art in the back while the ones fired in front found the agent's head. More bullets pierced Lady Thanatou, who left Elvie to snap the attacker's neck. As Art's back-shooter approached, Ellie kicked hard at a marble and toppled it.

Crunch.

With the shooter flattened and spreading fresh blood on the ground, Ellie sensed Art falling on the shooter in front, her limbs jerking from possible damage to her brain. But Art's hand closed on the man's face, smothering him. That left one last attacker to subdue, and as Ellie regained her feet, she could only watch as Stavros grabbed Elvie and stabbed her in the neck with his syringe.

⚊

Art felt the remains of her right eye dribble down her cheek as she sought to subdue the struggling shootist beneath her. She could still see from her remaining eye — the eerie, floating euphoria gained from body-shock, aside — but her left limbs were not obeying her. Helia came beside Art, her breath harsh, and bludgeoned the man with a loose stone. When the man groaned, stilling, Helia hit him again.

Art put a hand out to halt Helia before she killed him. Then she attempted to rise, and Helia dropped her stone to help her. Art felt that her ability to think seemed intact, but control of her body was severely impaired. She attempted to gaze around the garden.

She looked to Ellie, who stood far right of an assailant holding tight to Elvie, a syringe piercing her neck. Lady Thanatou stood to the left, bloodied, but with a hand raised to her mask, the attendant Adara behind her. Art herself was centre yet farthest, and she knew neither of the other women could risk the man squeezing the syringe's plunger before he could be stopped. With great effort, Art willed her head to heal.

Her repairing brain pushed the lodged bullet out her shot eye socket. It landed with a splat on the ground, and the bullets stuck in her chest began to move up her gullet. Helia held her as tremors shook her body.

"That man is Stavros," Helia whispered. "And—"

"Remove your hand from your mask or she dies, monster!" Stavros yelled, his fingers poised upon the syringe's plunger.

Elvie let out a pained cry, and Lady Thanatou slowly lowered her hand.

"Vlorp," Art said, vomiting up the bullets from her chest. Ectoplasm and bullets splattered on the garden paving, and Stavros turned in her and Helia's direction. "I know your powers, demon! Turn invisible, and I will kill her! Move one inch from the woman next to you, and I will kill her!" he cried.

Art tried not to move, though she still spasmed, and discarded her thought of attempting ghosting.

"Unhappy man," Adara accused. "Why do you threaten a harmless blind girl?"

"Chorus of one," Stavros said. "Shut your mouth."

"Your wife was dying, Stavros," Adara said. "Tuberculosis. You could not let her go, and she did not know what more to do for you. Her marble was her gift."

"It was no gift!" he yelled. "Death is not *her* gift." He gestured with his chin at Lady Thanatou. "The monster should suffer as we all have, this I swore on my wife's stone body!"

He stepped back, forcing Elvie to face Lady Thanatou. She cried out again in his grip, the syringe deep in her straining neck. Art moved one foot forward, gauging her body's control. She tottered and Helia helped to hold her erect.

"You," Stavros said to Lady Thanatou. "You who are our *pharmakon*, both our remedy and poison. And we who are your sick, your *pharmakos*!" He laughed. "Are you so fond of your present sacrifice?" He gave Elvie a shake. "No doubt she will die soon, just like all your companions. Simple to love, simple to ease the suffering of, like any ill pet, forever honoured in your precious collection. She can easily die right now!"

"W—what?" Elvie gasped.

"The blood of your right side cures, the one from the left kills. Which kind do you think is in this syringe, taken from your slain sister, Euryale?"

Lady Thanatou took a step forwards.

"Don't move! You withheld life from my dying wife—you whose blood can even resurrect the *dead*. You could have saved her!"

"Release Elvie," Lady Thanatou bade in a quiet voice.

"Watch her die!" He held Elvie tighter and she shrieked.

"Coward," Adara said. "Twice you've tried to kill our lady with her sister's blood. Twice you failed, and now would take the life of an innocent?"

"Silence!" he said. "You are all demons!"

He looked from Lady Thanatou to Art, and Art froze, watching his hand with the syringe. Lady Thanatou took one more step, and Stavros swung back.

"Holy Virgin!" he cried. "Our Lady, august Queen of Heaven, most Holy Mother, send thy angels to crush the enemy before us! All ye holy angels and archangels, help and defend us! Holy angels and archangels, keep and protect us! *Bind* this monster, who I name Terror and Dread! Petrify this beast, known as the Awful One, the Gorgon! Smite the daughter of Phorkys and Keto, *Medousa!*"

Lady Thanatou froze, two steps away from Stavros and Elvie. Her snood rustled.

Serpents shot from the parted snood like arrows, straight for Stavros's face. Their wide mouths sank fangs into his flesh. Two golden snake heads bit down on his staring eyes. They withdrew with hisses and darting tongues, and Stavros slumped. Elvie wrenched the syringe from her neck and sank to the floor with him, burdened by his weight.

Lady Thanatou reached for her mask.

Art turned herself and Helia away, just as Ellie dropped a heavy veil around her own head and Adara shielded her eyes. Art covered Helia's eyes with one spasming hand and held the other aloft, looking within the hand mirror with her good eye. There, she saw the Gorgon's head in profile. Greek nose, full lips, pronounced cheekbones, and arched, black brow. Shining golden snakes curled about the striking outline. Lady Thanatou's bright blue eye rolled to the side and noted her, the orb's gaze flashing. She reached down to where Elvie knelt.

"No! Let me be!" Elvie cried, wrenching from Thanatou's grasp. The lady started, surprised, and Elvie struggled to her feet.

Elvie heard the strike of snakes, their muscular bodies vibrating around her face. Stavros gasped, and when his grip slackened, sibilant hisses surrounded her, then withdrew. She reached up for the needle and pulled it out with a pained cry, then fell with the heavy weight of the man. Beneath her hands were a slack jaw and a warm face, covered in seeping pinpricks. She pulled back and tried to wipe her shaking hands. Then the scent of roses cloaked her and she felt the sculptress's touch.

"No! Let me be!" she shouted. A great pain, deep and abiding, sprang wide within her. Inside, she could only cry: *Liar! Liar!*

She rose and stumbled over Stavros in her haste to get away. "Ellie!" she cried out. "*Ellie!* Take me home, please!"

"But is she masked?" Ellie called out.

"Don thy mask, Friend," Art said, her tone warning. After a moment, she spoke again. "Aye, Ellie, all is safe."

Ellie's arm pressed against hers. She grabbed it. They began walking, and Elvie hurried to keep pace with Ellie's fast strides.

"Elvie!" Lady Thanatou called behind her.

"You are a deceiver!" Elvie said.

"You are a child," the lady answered, her voice sharp and near. Snakes hissed. "This is what I am. You knew full well before that man appeared."

"I know you've the power to kill; I've thought on it! And now what? You like your companions a *certain* way?" Her voice rose. "Then it is true, your death cult—your work, as *death goddess*. I'm 'perfect' for you, you said. I will not be a part of it, especially if what *he* said was—if I'm—"

Her words stuck; she could not voice it. Once announced, it would be reality. Somehow, her stick found her hand. The sun's warmth fell upon her face; they had exited the house for the driveway. A horse clopped near. She wondered if the sculptress dared follow with her snake hair revealed. Yet right then, Elvie hardly cared. She pressed at the pain returning between her eye sockets, then straightened.

"I am life!" she cried. "I will live! And you—stay with your stones and dead!"

Ellie helped her into the open cab.

"Art and I will call upon you later," she heard Helia say with concern to Ellie just as their hansom cab pulled away.

"I know you can sense it, Ellie," Elvie said dully, holding her head.

Ellie stiffened beside her, and Elvie was too weary to ask when Ellie had planned to tell her. She recalled all of Ellie's clumsy ruses to have her see her doctor. No one liked to be death's messenger, not even death's goddess.

"I'm ill again, aren't I?" she said.

Ellie remained silent, the horse's steady hooves Elvie's only answer.

"That's why she can't promise to keep me safe," Elvie said. "And she, with the power to make me safe, if the talk of good and evil blood were true. If she even cared." She put her hands to her face and let herself cry.

—⌘—

She fell ill thereafter.

All her classes were cancelled or taken over by other boarders. She handed in the last of her stockings quota and knit no more. She tried to work on her clays, but her head wouldn't allow it. Something more was wrong within her skull, for the pressure reached her nose, her ears. It ruined her ability to stand upright to finish her *Aphrodite*. Mrs Darby said she was experiencing what the sighted called "dizzy," and Elvie grew weaker.

She had to take to bed, where the simple act of reading could not calm her or lessen the pressure. Ellie visited, and Elvie knew it was very bad when Ellie sat beside her to hold her hand.

"Elvie," Ellie said, worry in her tone. "Yer uncle, the doctor, is below."

"He can't help; he knows and I know, the day has come. Make certain he says nothing to my brother. Intimidate him for me, Ellie!"

"Elvie . . . if yer in pain, perhaps he can give you somethin'—"

"I've a heart rent in two," Elvie said. "What medicine may ease such pain? And perhaps my misery is causing the malignancy to grow and grow, so fast. Nothing may stop that."

———

Helia sat at her table in the Blue Vanda and typed, uncaring that other patrons looked disapprovingly upon her cigarette smoking and debris of discarded paper balls. The din of the Royal Aquarium echoed in the great dome and was fitting background noise while she mulled her words. The story of Rose Batts required subtle handling, an aspect to reportage she was not accustomed to. Her forté was not the social reform exposé, informing the public of the plight of ordinary, forgotten, and impoverished girls. She'd too much personal history associated with that, as Annie Le Bon knew. Helia hit the return lever and tried typing a new line. Then she raised her head, feeling that something needed her attention.

Ellie stood near, blackthorn in hand, with a look on her face that gave Helia immediate concern.

"It's Elvie," Ellie said. "She's sickened so quickly."

———

An hour later, Helia stood with Art outside Brompton's Little Oratory. Holy Trinity Church sat near, a mere stone's throw away while labourers worked within the foundations already laid for the true oratory. Art turned her gaze from the bell tower of Trinity for the façade of the little chapel.

"The many houses of God," Art said, her tone thoughtful.

An electric vehicle hummed as it approached. Helia and Art watched Lady Thanatou, seated in her one-woman buggy, smoothly direct it up the drive and round the side of the chapel. She disappeared from their view.

Helia let out a breath. She couldn't fathom why an ancient Greek creature would want to meet at a tiny Catholic church overshadowed by its imposing Anglican neighbour, but she doubted she could ever guess at the whims of a two-thousand-year-old woman's mind. Art look down at her, her gaze as always, attentive and receptive.

"Would thee like me to speak to her?" she asked.

"No, dear, she must hear this from me," Helia said, placing a reassuring hand on Art's arm. "But thank you for being here, dear Art. I don't think she would have agreed to meet otherwise."

Art picked up Helia's hand and kissed it upon the knuckles. "I will be good, and not turn invisible and eavesdrop. But if I do not hear from thee in less than ten minutes, Helia, I will come for thee."

"It will be sooner," Helia promised. She entered the chapel's doors.

When the doors shut, she breathed again, smelling melted candles, the remnants of burnt frankincense, and the polished wood of pews, and wished her heart would calm and not beat so frantically. She jumped when she noticed the ceramic holy water font near her, bearing its simple golden cross, then clapped a hand over her mouth to stifle her nervous giggle.

Lady Thanatou stood in a shadowed side aisle of the chapel, beside the booth of a confessional. She slipped into its door and it shut behind her.

Helia hurried across the nave, the masked side of her face burning as she passed the white altar and its purple cloths. She balled her hands into fists and addressed the curse she harboured.

"Shut it—shut it—shut it!" she hissed.

An old woman rose from where she knelt. She crossed herself as she stared in fright at Helia, then departed. Helia dropped her fists.

Of course, Helia thought. *This is why she led me here.*

She breathed and ignored her infection's roiling discontent. Calming, she went to the confessional and entered.

In the darkness of the small space, Helia knelt on the cushion facing the carved wooden screen. She could spy the outline of Lady Thanatou within, her monocle dully gleaming. The lady did not face the screen but sat in profile, the drawn eye on her golden mask blankly impassive. Helia clasped her hands before the lattice.

"Once, I did terrible things," she said, "and my love went to prison for them. She suffered and died there, thanks to me. But I could not let her stay dead. I did not have to look far to find a way to cheat her of death, and unlike Tiberius Teegan, I *chose* to be selfish.

"Why are we given access to such power?" she asked. "Why do we get to decide: life or death?

"I bought her a second life, and that too has a terrible price. It is a life everlasting. And this gift, this curse given my love—how can a woman keep her good heart and risk feeling, caring, losing, as the years go on? How can a woman allow heartbreaks forever?

"You must understand. For yours is a story told long before Homer sang. You have the power to save life and to resurrect. Once you must have done so. And now . . . you do not."

Helia listened and heard nothing through the screen.

"The price you must have paid," she said, her tone soft, "and I suspect you still pay. Centuries have gone. What do you think of us now, who are mere blinks to you? Or are we? Do we still matter? Can you still love us?

"And if you still love," she said, "is that not worth trying one more time?"

She heard swift movement, and the door next to her shut.

"For everything," Helia whispered.

CHAPTER FOURTEEN

In the Institute of the Blind, where Mrs Darby boiled sheets, and medicine bottles accumulated on a bedside table, the blind sat in the drawing room and shared speculations in hushed voices. Elvie lay in her bed, alone, weak, and ill, and raged.

"Little *kore*," she said angrily. "Little marble for your collection." She was weary of tears, yet she cried more. She never knew that tear ducts could produce so much water.

Fool, she thought. *Is she worth such self-pity? There isn't much time left! Live!*

But what weighted down her skull and made her body ill intertwined with her misery. She missed the sculptress like a body halved. She wanted to hear how the new sculptures were advancing, wondered how the sculptress felt, if she'd found another sad subject to copy. She craved her touch, her voice, her scent, her words, wanted to kiss her, know her, touch her face. How was it possible to lose so much to someone?

She could not remain angry; she could never blame the

sculptress for her death. The malignancy within her brain was her true killer.

And if not for an uncle learned in modern surgery, Elvie should have been dead as a very small child. She'd lived a charmed life; it was what everyone had said of her; she'd outraced death for so long. Sarah would say that Elvie was returning at last to her goblin folk. She thought about that— for if a Gorgon could be real, then so could such weird kin—and dreamt a great, silent goblin presence weighed her down, sinking her into her bed, while strange little things snatched at her fingers.

"Elvie, we should send word to your brother," Ellie said when she sat once more by her side.

"No! Ellie, he will stop my money, even before I'm gone. And he was such a selfish miser to begin with, trying to deny me my sum when our parents died. He should not enjoy a penny sooner."

"Oh. I do agree, er . . . which of us ought to pretend to be you, then?"

"Well, if Mrs Darby is agreeable, accept the money as myself for as long as you can. I'll have to be buried sometime."

After that conversation, Elvie felt too ill to think on anything further. Ellie tried to comfort her with reading aloud Elvie's favourite books, and Sarah with passages of the Bible, but she could not listen, not with her ears and face afflicted by the invisible vise her head seemed screwed into. She only knew that time passed by Mrs Darby's attempts to have her fed, but the broth she ingested came back up again. The headache powders were all that she could stand, and the tears returned when she realised: it was happening too fast.

I wish I'd more time, she thought.

In the midst of drifting into, or out of, sleep, she thought she heard commotion—Mrs Darby?—and wondered if bandits had come at last to prey on the weak. Or a stern man of the cloth had arrived, especially at Sarah's insistence, so that Elvie might finally earn her admittance into heaven or the horrors of hell. She wanted neither. She wanted her soul to go to Hades where she might, at the end of time, meet her love there.

Death is when you sleep, she thought. She slept.

Roses; she became aware of roses. The Anatolian rose, borne on frankincense and myrrh. Elvie reached for her rose woman, but her arm was leaden, her grasp weak. She felt the clasp of the sculptress's roughened, warm hand and deemed it right that her touch should guide her over the threshold into forever.

The sculptress leaned close, her lips at her ear.

"Once, I attempted my sister's resurrection," she whispered. "Her name was Medousa."

She pressed closer, and the words that entered Elvie surrounded her with sound.

"I am Euryale," she said.

Euryale. The name sank inside Elvie like fingers in warm, soft bread. Within, Elvie shouted in realisation. Her heart lifted in song.

"Please accept my gift," the sculptress said.

"For . . . ?" Elvie whispered.

"It is simply my gift."

Elvie felt sleep weigh her; she was the sun, disappearing.

Yes, she tried to say.

She felt the sculptress's fingertips at her lids. The lady gently held them open.

Liquid splashed into Elvie's eye sockets, hot and burning.

It ran into the crevices of her eye muscles and tissues and spilt down her cheeks. Drops touched her lips and entered her mouth: blood. The piercing taste was liquor that ignited.

Her lids shut, holding the hot blood to her, and its warmth throbbed. A fire ran through her brain, beating, pounding.

"I hear . . . your heart," she whispered. The sculptress's thumbs soothed the corners of her shut lids. She lost consciousness to a vision within the depths of her brain that she'd never known before: it seemed the opposite of "dark."

Elvie burned like one poisoned; in her eye sockets, in her head. Her body was a furnace, and she thought she must have died despite Lady Thanatou's gift and gone to hell. Then she was freezing, which she thought might be the other hell. Hands held her down or soothed her brow, and all the hands were not the roughened texture or firm strength of the sculptress. She breathed and tasted cinnamon, frankincense, and myrrh, and felt the air transformed. She drank spring water, light, pure, and crisp. She vomited. Women sang songs she did not know, in a language that formed shapes in her brain as strings of *Aphrodites* and *discoboluses*. Then she felt Thana.

"Hello," Elvie said. *Was the blood hard for you too?*

She stopped burning, freezing, and vomiting and slept like one dead, knowing Thana was near.

She woke to sun on her face and a clear, though lightheaded, awareness and knew it was morning. Her head's constant pressure was gone.

"Miss," Corrina said from beside her bed, "good morning."

"Good morning," Elvie croaked, and those words were all she could manage.

Recovery, she thought as Corrina helped her from the bed and into a chair. It was all Elvie wanted to focus on and not whether her reprieve was only that, and her malignancy, having been battled, merely lay subdued. She did not voice such fear. Besides Corrina there were several women who attended to her in her little room, much to her surprise. They drew a bath for her, smelling of sweet lavender, right in her room, and the receptacle, she was told, was fashioned of copper. Elvie sat in the penetrating warmth and felt like a cooked chicken. They saw to the care of her sick bed, stripping it of sheets, and flung the windows open, bringing in cool, sharp air. Birds sang.

"Where might—Lady Thanatou?" she asked, her voice shaky.

"She is here, miss," Corrina assured as she washed Elvie. "You must regain full health first, and then she will come for you."

Despite the bath's warmth, Elvie shivered at the thought. She would play Andromeda chained upon her rock if that would make the sculptress come.

The next days passed in sleeping and eating while she gained strength, clarity, and a little body weight. They fed her soup and fish, and when she became stronger, roasted chicken, broad beans, eggs, figs, olives, bread dipped in olive oil, barley cakes, and delicious honey cakes. They persuaded her to drink honeyed wine, which she was relieved to find well-watered. She marvelled at the sheer bounty and the thought that Mrs Darby had given up the kitchen and several rooms for the sculptress's people. If fellow boarders and children came to visit, they kept to the doorway (or perhaps the attendants made them do so) and briefly voiced their cheery well-wishes, for Corrina did not want her to overtire. One day Elvie rose by herself and touched all her neglected clays. Those present in her room let her be, though she felt the warmth of their approval, and Corrina led her back to bed again, made with sheets smelling of lavender. They bathed her daily and Elvie felt that if any slumbering malignancy wished to reemerge, it was thoroughly washed away.

Corrina had dressed Elvie in a freshly laundered chemise (one she thought new, for it did not feel like one of her own) and was putting her back in bed when Ellie entered.

"Ellie!" Elvie said in gladness, for she recognised her friend's step. She held out hands for her, and Ellie took hold of one and laid long, lean fingers upon her face. Her touch remained there a while.

"Ellie?" Elvie said.

"All is well, Elfin," Ellie said softly. "Perfectly well."

Elvie hugged her, and Ellie gripped her tight enough to make her lose breath. Then Ellie straightened.

"Well, now. 'Ere's yer miracle maker."

The scent of roses filled Elvie's senses. She heard many bodies abruptly move.

"Thank you all fer prostatin' yerselves, but I'll be leavin' now," Ellie announced to the room and walked away.

Elvie held her hands out, yearning, and suddenly the sculptress was there. Hot, firm hands accepted hers, and Elvie heard heavy skirts gather on the floor. She felt a kiss on her fingertips, and Elvie realised with a blush that the position of the hands meant that Lady Thanatou knelt before her.

"Oh my, well I—oh," Mrs Darby said in hushed

astonishment from the doorway. Then there was a heavy sound of flesh hitting the floor, accompanied by laboured breathing. It sounded as though Mrs Darby was also kneeling. "Hail Mary, Mother of God, a miracle must have happened for all to be bowing so," she exclaimed. "Amen!"

The lady issued an order in Greek. Elvie heard the shuffle of people rising, and then Mrs Darby exclaiming more while being helped to her feet. People exited and the door shut. The room then felt bereft of presence, except for Elvie and the sculptress.

"You stayed away," Elvie said softly. She did not mean it as an accusation. She was concerned.

"I wanted the healing to work, Elvie," the sculptress said. Her hand ran along Elvie's forehead and down her cheek. "And your friend confirms that it has."

"I don't understand. You brought back those turned to stone with your blood. Ellie had said. Why did you worry?"

"Death is my true gift, Elvie, restoring life is not. I did not cause your illness and therefore could not simply take it away." Her thumb caressed Elvie's forehead. "Asclepius was a healer, unselfish and pure. To perform the miracle, the blood must be a gift. I must tell myself I don't want you."

Elvie took the lady's hands and held them tightly.

"That you are not mine," the sculptress said.

"You let me go," Elvie said. "You let pride go."

"I let more than that go," Lady Thanatou whispered, and hot drops fell on Elvie's hands.

"Then we could part, right now, and you would never pursue me," Elvie said. "And I've the power of your true name. I, Elvie, may command you, Lady Thanatou, and make you my slave!"

The sculptress turned rigid.

"Do you still want me?" Elvie asked innocently.

"Elvie," the sculptress said. "Why do you test me so?"

Elvie hung her head, though she smiled. "I am sorry. That was wicked of me."

"Insult me again, and you will have to gift me your blood and a secret," the lady said, her tone mild.

"I am so very sorry," Elvie said. She felt the sculptress's face and cheeks and thought her tears had ceased. Finding her hands again, she kissed them and repeated her apology with each press of her lips, loving both hands. She took in one of the roughened fingers and gave it a wet kiss. She sucked upon it.

The sculptress suddenly grabbed her and kissed her on the mouth. She removed her mask and kissed her again. The viperine hair rustled, and Elvie felt the weight of the snood against her hands as she held Lady Thanatou's face. The fabric loosened, and warm, serpentine bodies entangled her fingers, her wrists. Elvie shuddered and grew light-headed.

The snakes released her, and the lady took Elvie's breath away with more kisses. She pulled Elvie's chemise off, and when Elvie felt the sculptress's gaze upon her, she lost all thoughts of propriety. She'd brushed death and earned the right to be bold. She basked, a wanton Eve, and felt higher appreciation given when a silk sleeve touched her throat and slowly ran down the length of her trembling body. The soft sound of fabric on her flesh, measuring her and knowing her, was so very different from fabric knowing stone.

When Elvie felt the sculptress's bared body pressed against her own, desperation twined with the need to affirm: she was alive, *alive!* The final sleep had been averted, and the paralysing fear that had diminished her, lingering in her organs and soul, would be ejected. She urged the sculptress's touch to confirm: her body was not death's but once more *hers.*

Haphê, she demanded.

Joy bloomed when she shook from a pleasure and beauty she hadn't known. Gasping, she shared breath, heat, ecstatic love; all were the bubbles made within that rose, and the sculptress made it so. When breath and pleasure gentled, Elvie laughed in the sculptress's arms, and the need to give praise broke from her lips. She embraced her lover and sang:

> Now shall my inward joys arise,
> And burst into a Song;
> Almighty Love inspires my Heart,
> And Pleasure tunes my Tongue.

Lady Thanatou rocked her, and Elvie fell against her, laughing more. She touched her empty eye sockets and raised both hands and face to the ceiling.

> Lady on her thirsty Sion-Hill
> Some Mercy-Drops has thrown,
> And solemn Oaths have bound her Love
> To show'r Salvation down.

She stopped singing when the lady blew into her throat, making a rude noise.

The boarders gathered in the drawing room heard Elvie's muted laughter.

"She changed the words again," Sarah said as she wove a basket next to the drawing room's low fire.

Ellie continued to read her book. "It's 'er favourite hymn, Sarah. She may do what she likes."

"I'm glad she feels well again. I give thanks to Our Lord. She ought to be baptised, though," Sarah said.

"I'll fetch our hymn books," Mrs Darby said, rising from her rocking chair. "We—we should sing our thanks. Oh, we should. Thanks be to God! Oh, praise Him." She departed.

Ellie smiled and pretended to read as she noted the silent, slow descent down the staircase of one of Lady Thanatou's attendants. The woman carried a brass incense burner on a chain. She swung it, and smoke from the burning frankincense and myrrh wafted. Ellie knew that the attendant had been filling all the rooms and grounds of the institute with the scent.

"'Praise Her,' y'mean," Ellie murmured.

Elvie felt the cold of night grow, but the sculptress was a hot, demanding, considerate, and loving presence in her bed. She covered Elvie with blankets. Then swept them aside again. Elvie slept, revelled, slept, and revelled again.

Sometimes she touched her forehead, searching for the familiar pain, but the pressure never returned, as if it had never been.

"You held both my eye sockets open," Elvie said in wonder. "But where did your blood come from?"

"My tongue, Elvie. I pierced its right side."

"Oh." Elvie held the lady to her. "I love your tongue."

The sculptress ran that tongue down her body, and then Elvie could speak no more.

She wanted to say, "How bold you are, seducing me right here in the Institute of the Blind." She wondered how much

Mrs Darby was given to ignore what was happening behind Elvie's closed door.

In the morning, the sculptress flung Elvie's curtains wide open when she woke to the world also waking. Morning warmth filled the room, and Elvie wondered what "glowing" was like, for perhaps she felt just like that right then, inside her skin and thrumming life with an equally alive, languid body joining once more with her own. The sun itself lived in her room.

"Your fellow boarders persist in listening at the door," Lady Thanatou said. "Come live with me."

"Yes," Elvie agreed. She recalled the request she'd made in the marble garden, when she'd thought of what a dangerous and possibly capricious creature she was throwing herself upon. One who, like the lioness, might accidentally maul its precious lamb. But none of those had been true concerns, especially when based on the accusations of a vengeful man. Her death goddess had chosen life; had chosen her, Elvie.

She moved hands up her lover's back, and sleek snake bodies twined with her hands and wrists again, capturing them. They rubbed their heads against her. Very carefully, she disengaged and listened to the soft hisses.

Regardless of the viperine hair, the practical matters of a relationship with a goddess needed considering. Later, she might tell her: *I am independent. I'm not your courtesan, and I shall go where I please and I'll have the friends I like—though my heart may already be enslaved to you.* Foolish terms to express to one born of sea gods, but Elvie was an Englishwoman. She hoped their circumstance, if agreeable, would last more than a month, a year. Forever.

She traced the large areola mammae on the soft breast beneath her and then started, gripping the sculptress's shoulders.

"That was *you*," she accused. "You in the garden, with your callipygian body and mons veneris showing!"

The sculptress kissed her, stifling her own laughter against Elvie's mouth.

Yet even her lady's wonderful, shapely bottom and kisses could not distract Elvie from her working mind. She had so many questions, and they were still strangers, after all.

"When that man said he killed Euryale," she began.

"That was Stheno, Elvie, and she is not dead," Euryale said. "Though she is very, very angry."

"Oh." Elvie was uncertain if she'd like to meet the Gorgon said to be the most fearsome of the sisters. Or Medusa, who might be resurrected still or simply undead. "My, you both like to confuse people, though I now understand why you do. Would his prayer have worked then, had he named you correctly?"

"I have yet to meet this Holy Virgin. If she or her angels had come . . . perhaps we could have discussed matters before fighting."

"Yes, have them sit for tea," Elvie said. She ran her hand up Euryale's hip. "The Virgin aside, do the others of your pantheon exist too? I mean . . . the self-important ones."

"Perhaps," Euryale said.

"I must avoid saying names out loud. I would not like to be visited by the one who wore your sister's face on her aegis." Elvie smiled. "But as I may sometimes speak of her, I shall simply call her Flashing Eyes or Apple Face."

Elvie smiled more as Euryale's body shook from suppressed laughter. Elvie trailed her hands up, and Euryale helped her fingers glide up the slopes of her breasts—breasts Elvie found quite perfect and far more ample than her own—and paused her touch at the throat. She traced the scar.

"Perhaps you might tell me, sometime," she whispered, "of how you outwitted those who did this."

Euryale brought Elvie's fingers up to touch her lips and the smile there. Elvie found sharp canines and understood then why the sculptress's smile made its sound. She felt the curve of Euryale's cheekbones and thought the grin triumphant. Beneath the left eye she followed a trailing scar, thick and jagged.

"That eye is growing back," Euryale said before Elvie could ask. Elvie's fingertips followed the scar over a shut eyelid halved by the damage. Farther up she found the arched brow, also split in two. She brought her lips to the scar and kissed it, hearing the serpents' tongues flick.

"I assume who did this no longer lives?" she asked.

"They do not."

Elvie shivered. Perhaps the ones who'd harmed Euryale had considered themselves heroes; monster killers. But she remembered the syringe plunged into her neck.

"What might I call you?" Elvie suddenly asked. "Consider me more than impertinent when I refuse to address you as 'mistress.' Or, like a contrary Ganymede, decline to carry your drinking cups."

"But mine are such beautiful cups, Elvie," Euryale said lightly. She tickled Elvie and made her laugh.

Euryale the Far-Roaming, Elvie thought, warmth imbuing her. *How glad I am that you are not the Queen.*

"In English, I have taken the name Envy," Euryale said, and Elvie felt another smile beneath her fingers. She ran her hands back down and found Euryale's hands.

"Envy. Envy and Elvie." Elvie turned to face the windows and the sun's warmth. "Very well."

The end.

Round the margin roll'd, A fringe of serpents hissing guards the gold: Here all the terrors of grim War appear, Here rages Force, here tremble Flight and Fear, Here storm'd Contention, and here Fury frown'd, And the dire orb portentous Gorgon crown'd.

—The Iliad, Homer, translation by Alexander Pope, 1899

CHARACTER KEY

(in order of appearance):

Elvie Chaisty (also called Elfin): a blind boarder at the Institute of the Blind

Ellie Hench (also Petronella Hench): a blind stick for hire

Mrs Darby: sighted housekeeper at the Institute of the Blind

Sarah: a blind boarder at the Institute of the Blind

Alan: a blind boarder at the Institute of the Blind

Mrs Husher-King: suffragette spokeswoman and one of Ellie's clients

Clyde Barlew: custodian at the British Museum and Elvie's male pest

Sgt Trilby: war veteran and souvenir photographer

Artifice: artificial ghost and agent of HRH Secret Commission

Atlas: quake maker and agent of HRH Secret Commission

Mr Hands of Thunder: thunder maker and agent of HRH

Secret Commission
Jim Dastard: animated skull and agent of HRH Secret Commission
Manon: woman in residence at the Vesta and companion to Artifice
Helia Skycourt: journalist for the *Times*
Corrina, Ahmet, and Alexys: attendants of the Thanatou household
Adara: keeper of the Thanatou household
Tiberius Teegan: wealthy American
Dolly Teegan: daughter to Tiberius
Stavros: vengeful Greek man
Lady Envy Thanatou: sculptress; also known as Medousa, daughter of Phorkys and Keto, and also by her true name, Euryale
Miss Annie Le Bon: social reformer, activist, publisher, and writer
Countess Olgfrey: evil woman
Rose Batts: unfortunate captive of Countess Olgfrey

ANCIENT GREEK LANGUAGE KEY

Haphê: (noun) Touch
Khaíre: (singular) Good afternoon/evening
Aspázdomai: "Welcome"
Despoina: Lady or mistress of the house.
Hypíaine: (singular) good morning, good-bye, good night
Hetaera: One of a class of highly cultivated courtesans in ancient Greece (Merriam-Webster).
Haptesthai: (verb) to touch
Hesperisma: a light meal.
Kala: Good (Not ancient Greek, but casual enough for the context used.)
Kardia: heart, mind, as in the seat of thought and emotion, not the organ itself (Strong's Greek).
Kore: The standing statue of a maiden, found in Greek sculptural art beginning 700 BCE (with prototypes found in Egyptian and Mesopotamian art). It is the female counterpart to the standing youth, *kouros*, and both are idealisations of young beauty.
Pharmakos: the person often already condemned to death sacrificed in ancient Greece as a means of purification or atonement for a city or community (Merriam-Webster). Besides the sacrifice being a criminal, this person may also be disabled or a slave.
Pharmakon: the present interpretation of this word is that

it may mean both remedy (cure) and poison. If the visage of the Gorgon (Medusa) has an apotropaic function, it can be seen as a *pharmakon*, both the cure and the evil itself, and also simultaneously, the *pharmakos*—the sacrifice to atone for evil. (*Companion to Literary Myths, Heroes, and Archetypes*, edited by Pierre Brunel, published 1996 by Routledge).

Here is one paper defining *pharmakon*:
http://faculty.arts.ubc.ca/pmahon/pharmakon.html

And another:
http://flutuante.wordpress.com/2009/08/01/pharmakon-the-cure-or-the-poison/

AUTHOR NOTES

Timeline:

Medusa occurs after the events of *Everlife*, which puts it around May of 1880. The events of *Risen, Bones,* and *Everlife* happen in March and April of 1880. Ellie's first appearance and fight with Art happened in *Bones*.

The British Museum:

In winter of 1992, I visited the British Museum and after enjoying the Greek and Egyptian antiquities descended to the lower level. I entered a large room where the sculptures, all Roman and some duplicates, seemed to be stored in a haphazard fashion. Hardly anyone was there except for an art student or two, sketching, and I remembered that it was hard to manoeuvre in. Some of the copies were painfully mundane. I was struck by how the mystique of sculpture was missing; the majesty and timelessness of stone and the opportunity to appreciate form under optimal lighting. It was all just a hodgepodge.

Whether that was Room 83, 84, 85, or some other room, I don't know, and I doubt I took (analog) pictures of such a dull setting. What online photos exist of rooms 83, 84, and 85 show far better organisation, lighting, and spacing than I recall. But for Elvie and this story, I took the liberty of giving her the room I remember, faulty as that memory might be. I also gave her access to marbles that probably never existed as multiple copies, so one might consider my

Room 84 either magical or very much an alternate reality. To read more of the British Museum Elvie would have known, refer to: *The Dickens's Dictionary of London* by Charles Dickens Jr, published 1879.

Blindness and haptic perception:

I tried to keep in mind the concepts the always blind would not know or the longtime blind would have forgotten and then removed them from the writing: depth perception (like the idea of a very far distance, or how a house seems very tiny far away, yet is still the size of a house). Colour, of course, and metaphors and emotions like "dark mood," "bright disposition," etc. We sighted are really dependent on describing abstract things and our environment in terms of light and dark. We're also very focused on how we use our gaze, head, body attitudes, and hand gestures to communicate and connect (the blind have no need to "look up" at someone taller, clasp their hands to beg, or nod yes or shake their head no, turn and face a person while speaking, and so on). I did my best to stay within haptic understanding for a longtime blind person, and it has been a pleasure trying to perceive the world as Elvie might know it.

When Elvie describes how raindrops would define the sculptress's studio to her, that was my homage to a beautiful documentary piece, "Notes on Blindness", a dramatisation of diary entries kept on cassette by writer and theologian John Hull, in which he describes—and which is so poetically portrayed in the film—a haptic perception of rain. That part begins at frame 9:30. http://youtu.be/0LoOWpWHMQw

ASMR (Autonomous Sensory Meridian Response):

I gave Elvie ASMR qualities because the stimulations for ASMR sensations are very tactile, auditory, and sensual. I made up the stimulation regarding fabric brushing stone (as far as I know). You can read more about ASMR, here: http://www.asmrlab.com/

Ellie's slang:
Ellie makes several slang references to male sexual organs. *Arbor vitae* is from the *1811 Dictionary of the Vulgar Tongue* by Francis Grose.

Helia and her quotes:
When Helia recites (replacing "the sails" with "her sails"):

> *Purple the sails, and so perfumed [that*
> *The winds were lovesick with them]*

It is from Act II, Scene two of Shakespeare's *Antony and Cleopatra*. It refers to the boat carrying Cleopatra to meet Antony for the first time, and the manner in which she seductively perfumed the sails of her ship.

And also when she recites:
> *Its horror and its beauty are divine.*

It is from "On the Medusa of Leonardo da Vinci in the Florentine Gallery" by Percy Bysshe Shelley, 1819.

When Helia says:
"According to Hesiod, the two older sisters, Stheno the

Mighty and Euryale the Far Springer were immortal, but Medusa the Queen was not . . . ."

This information about the three sisters is from the "Gorgon" entry of the *Encyclopaedia Britannica*. As the sisters' titles are based on translation, the variations that can be given are "Stheno the Forceful," "Euryale the Far Roaming," and "Medusa the Ruler,"

http://www.conservapedia.com/Gorgon
http://www.pantheon.org/articles/g/gorgons.html

The hymn Elvie sings after having sex:

And in which she changes the gender, is "Africa", by William Billings (this version, 1788), with lyrics by hymnodist Isaac Watts. I enjoy this joyous choral piece as sung by His Majestie's Clerkes, directed by Paul Hillier, from the album *Early American Choral Music Vol 1: Anthems and Fuging Tunes by William Billings*. The original lyrics are:

Now shall my inward joys arise,
And burst into a Song;
Almighty Love inspires my Heart,
And Pleasure tunes my Tongue.

God on his thirsty Sion-Hill
Some Mercy-Drops has thrown,
And solemn Oaths have bound his Love
To show'r Salvation down.

It is corny to break into song after sex, but that is Elvie, and I think reflects the unself-conscious and earnestly innocent attitudes of the time.

Symbolisms:

The Gorgon face is identified with the Evil Eye (*The Evil Eye: An Account of This Ancient and Widespread Superstition*, by Frederick Thomas Elworthy, published 1895), and the Eye is associated with destructive emotions like envy. Thus, I made *envy* one of Euryale's names.

I also linked Euryale with death, as with the frankincense and myrrh—not only are both fragrances symbolic of the ancient gods, but they're traditionally used in funerary rites—and when she names herself Thanatou, the female variant of Thanatos. Elvie is of course, linked with life. I found myself mistyping Elvie as "Elive" whilst writing this story, though her name also forms the anagram, "Evile." Her name is defined (in both Irish and English), as meaning "elfin."

Author's confession:

No one may appreciate the homage I'm about to confess to except perhaps people with 2D animation backgrounds or a deep appreciation of old Warner Bros cartoons. When I was pondering who my Medusa was going to be and how she would look, the Medusa character in "Porky's Hero Agency," 1937, came to mind. Having watched this cartoon as a child growing up and loving the wacky take on Greek hero myths and the monster known as Medusa, I take great joy in also creating a Gorgon who wears a photo-taking monocle and restores her victims via a syringe. So there you have it, the inspiration for Euryale and this rather mature story. I think she would like the cartoon.

More reference read for this story:

The Medusa Reader, edited by Marjorie Garber and

Nancy J. Vickers, published 2003 by Routledge

A Sense of the World: How a Blind Man Became History's Greatest Traveler, by Jason Roberts, published 2006 by Harper-Collins

Voyage Round the World Vol 1: Including Travels in Africa, Asia, Australasia, America etc., etc. From 1827 to 1832, by James Holman R. N. F. R. S., published 1834

Sex or Symbol?: Erotic Images of Greece and Rome, by Catherine Johns, published 1991 by British Museums Publications LTD

Public domain works can be found online at Project Gutenberg, Archive.org, and Google Books.

❖

A Glimpse Into:

Dark Victorian: BONES

"I Am Made of This"

Chapter One

A heavy fog rolled through London. Gaslights broke the dark as a hackney carriage drove down a deserted, cobbled street. Inside the carriage, Inspector Risk, a tall, dark-haired man with a thick moustache, sat and grimly regarded Dr. Speller, a bespectacled man with white mutton chop sideburns seated across from him. Dr. Speller moved his top hat around in his hands in excitement. The plainclothes sergeant, Barkley, took notes.

"It's Esther Stubbings, I'm sure of it," Dr. Speller said. "She is one of your victims."

"I've four bodies," Risk said. "Just skin and muscle. Full skeletons and organs entirely removed and no incisions made. Makes it hard to identify flattened faces. You're claiming that the organ almost sold to you tonight belonged to this Esther Stubbings, and therefore she's my victim."

"Well I've yet to identify the body, but the organ is unquestionably hers, Inspector, because I was the surgeon," Speller said. "Every woman's reproductive organs are different. I mean in shape. I recognized my own work, sir; I was the one who removed her second ovary. And Esther was alive and well just last week. The only way someone could harvest her organs is if she were murdered."

"And since we've her female vitals she has been," Risk said. "So this organ stealer, knowing you were a women's physician and vivisectionist, he comes to you for a sale."

"I vivisected only to learn," Speller said. "But for the most part I now merely dissect organs purchased solely from the Royal Surgical Sciences Academy."

"Indeed. The Academy. Which buys from men like the one you met tonight," Risk said. "Except this one knows to bring it directly to you. The dead woman I have is of the poor. We know it from her clothes. How can someone like that afford your services?"

"She can when she volunteers for the procedure," Speller said. "Like all members of the Academy, I'm a man of science and medicine. Not only do I use the skills learned, I practice new techniques that have successfully corrected female ailments. Esther Stubbings was on her way to becoming a fully healthy woman. And none of it, thankfully, by use of supernatural nonsense, claiming healing through organ transference and such!"

"But that's exactly what I have, doctor," Risk said. "Black arts surgery. Unless you can explain how four people have no skulls, eyes, or brains in their intact heads Without them having been pulled out of their nostrils."

"Not to mention," Sergeant Barkley said, "how His Royal Highness can be here with us today if not for supernatural medicine. Been nineteen years since he nearly died! We've a bunch of nonsense to thank."

Risk sighed while Speller glowered. The carriage came to a halt outside a lit station house.

"You stay here," Risk said to Speller. "We'll move on to the mortuary shortly for you to identify the woman. And you," he said to Barkley. "Stop talking. Let's go."

When Risk stepped down from the carriage he saw a young woman in an azure coat briskly leave the station entrance. Her brown hat was crooked, and wisps of dark hair escaped. Her skirts were cut high enough for the ankles of her boots to show. She wore a fitted leather mask on one side of her face. Helia Skycourt smiled at Risk and waved. She grabbed the penny-farthing resting against the station wall, took a running jump into the sidesaddle seat, and hit the treadle. The lantern in front of her wheel suddenly lit. She sped away into the dark and fog.

Risk watched her depart, incredulous.

"Damn journalist," he said. "Does she never sleep?"

Barkley stifled a yawn. They entered the station building.

"Inspector," Barkley said in a low voice as they walked into the dimly lit room. A uniformed man was behind the desk. "This case . . . it being supernatural. When will the Secret Commission start helping?"

"When we ask for it," Risk said curtly. "And not before. What do you have?" he said to the policeman who rose to greet him.

"Sir," the policeman said. He led them down a narrow hall. "The fellow Dr. Speller had us arrest will be brought out of his cell shortly. He refuses to speak and has answered no questions. The doctor told us the man only spoke once during the negotiating of the price of the organ and his accent was German."

"Looks a foreigner, then?" Risk asked. He followed the policeman into a room with a desk and chairs. He took the seat behind the desk while Barkley went to stand near the small, barred window.

"No sir," the policeman answered. "Well dressed, clean-faced, trimmed hair, tidy, hands that haven't seen hard labor. I'm guessing he's of the medical profession."

"Organ stealers usually are," Risk said. "Especially those who work in mortuaries." They heard shuffling steps approach. Two policemen brought a shackled man into the room. He was a slim fellow, tight-lipped and with one, nervous eye. His other eye had been removed, leaving a gaping, black socket. He did not bother to shut his eyelid. The men escorting him sat him in front of Risk.

"*Wie ist dein name?*" Risk said.

The man looked at him in surprise.

"The sooner you answer our questions," Risk said. "The sooner we catch who's doing these black arts surgeries. Because it isn't you, is it? So if you don't want the blame, give us someone else's name."

The man's posture became stiffer.

"That's four dead," Risk said staring into the man's one eye. "Is the gallows worth this surgeon? Give him up and you won't have to worry. Do your sentence and then get on with life, right?"

Risk watched the man; the prisoner seemed to grow even more frightened.

"Right," Risk said slowly. "Now who is he?"

A shot exploded, shattering the window behind the sergeant. Blood sprayed into Risk's face. The other men shouted and ran out the door. The prisoner sat slumped. Brain matter hung from the side of his forehead where the bullet had exited.

Shouts and running came from outside the station. Risk didn't bother looking out the broken window, knowing that all he'd see would be darkness and fog. He grimly pulled out his handkerchief and slowly wiped his face. Barkley touched the prisoner to see if he was still alive.

"Shall I send a message to the Secret Commission?" Barkley asked.

Risk stared at the dead man who'd just brought him an internal affairs nightmare.

"Do it," he said.

❖

Read more in Elizabeth Watasin's
Dark Victorian: Bones

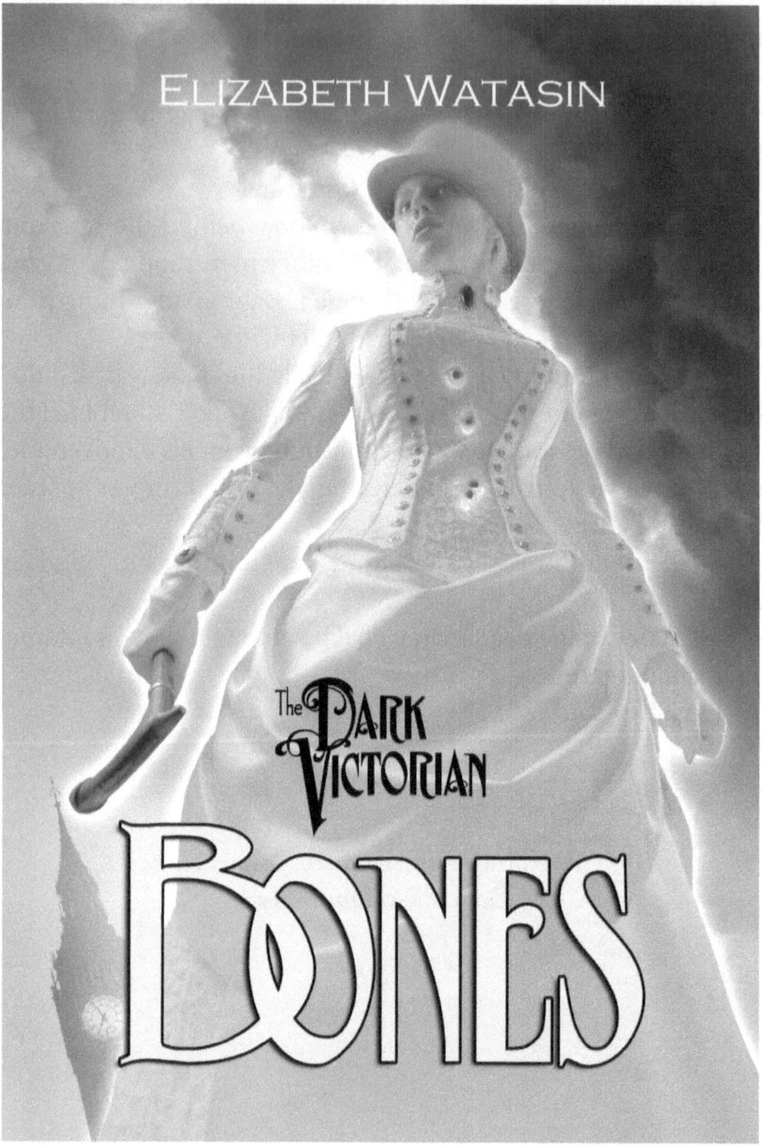
Elizabeth Watasin
The Dark Victorian
Bones

About The Author

Elizabeth Watasin is the author of the Gothic steampunk series *The Dark Victorian* and the creator/artist of the indie comics series Charm School. She has worked as an animation artist on thirteen Disney feature films, including *Beauty and the Beast, Aladdin, The Lion King,* and *The Princess and the Frog,* and has written for *Disney Adventures* magazine. She lives in Los Angeles with her black cat named Draw, busy bringing readers uncanny heroines in shilling shockers and adventuress tales.

Follow the news of her latest projects at A-Girl Studio.

www.a-girlstudio.com

Visit her online at:

https://www.facebook.com/groups/ElizabethWatasinsClubHecate

twitter.com/ewatasin

Look for Elizabeth's third gothic tale in The Dark Victorian series:

EVERLFE.

Then get ready for the third Dark Victorian penny dread: CIRCE.

KEEP
CALM
GHOST
AND
SKULL
ARE
HERE